SHERLOCK HOLMES &
THE RIPPER OF
WHITECHAPEL

SHERLOCK HOLMES &
THE RIPPER OF
WHITECHAPEL

M. K. WISEMAN

ISBN: 978-1-7344641-0-8 (hardcover)

ISBN: 978-1-7344641-1-5 (paperback)

ISBN: 978-1-7344641-2-2 (ebook)

Library of Congress Control Number: 2020905976

This is a work of fiction. Any references to real people, places, or historical events are used fictitiously. Other names, characters, places, descriptions, and events are products of the author's imagination or creations of Sir Arthur Conan Doyle and any resemblances to actual places or events or persons, living or dead, is entirely coincidental.

Edited by Sandra Hume and MeriLyn Oblad

Cover Illustration by Egle Zioma

Interior design created with Vellum

Published in the United States of America

1st edition: November 3, 2020

mkwisemanauthor.com

Contents:

1. Fifteen More
2. Dr. John. H. Watson
3. Dear Boss
4. To Catch The Devil
5. The Cry Of "Murder!"
6. One
7. Two
8. Developments
9. Bloody Apron
10. The Baker Street Irregulars
11. The Name Sherlock Holmes
12. Mary
13. Mrs. Watson
14. Funeral In Whitechapel
15. An Exercise In Futility
16. A Telegram And A Dark Vigil
17. From Hell
18. The Ending Of A Friendship
19. A Locked Door
20. The Devil's Fire
21. Death In The East End
22. Eulogy
Afterword
List of appearances

FIFTEEN MORE

CHAPTER 1

Three women had died under the Red Fiend's knife by the time I was consulted to investigate the series of murders occurring in Whitechapel during the latter half of 1888. I was, of course, aware of the horrific goings-on in London's East End. It was my business to know. I read the papers, and the clippings had been duly added to their appropriate files. I had no intention of participation, however, having considered various aspects of the attacks and deemed them unremarkable apart from their sheer brutality and the general mass hysteria these crimes had caused in that section of town. Watson had even come 'round in the early days of the case to counsel me against involvement.

Perhaps it was this exchange that ought to have aggravated my *pilious erectus* and stirred me from my couch at 221B. For John to come calling during his rounds to forward such a plea was curious enough. Since his marriage to Miss Morstan the prior autumn, his practice had grown to make heavy demands upon his time. I dare say even his wife was seeing very little of him. I certainly had not. But to have my friend, with his gentle spirit, warn me off assisting in the running down of the perpetrator of these particularly gruesome attacks ought to have inspired me to look all the more. I consider myself wholly to blame on that count. The Watson I knew would never have set justice aside nor asked it from another. In any event, it was Sir Charles Warren's card in my tray and his foot upon my stair that brought me into the singular affair at last.

"It's a bad business, Mr. Holmes." With that abrupt preamble, the hard-faced Commissioner of the Metropolitan Police leant forward through the open door to catch my hand in his. Mrs. Hudson had barely left us to our own when my visitor's military starch wilted, and I felt his grip grow slack.

"Sit. Please." I gestured to the couch and strode across the room to fetch brandy and glass.

He waved me off, and his eyes, begging that I say nothing of the temporary lapse, regained some of their sheen. "You know of the ghastly murders we've had over in Whitechapel?"

"I have some small knowledge of several recent events, yes."

The Commissioner grunted and hunted about his pocket for match and cigarette. With a pause to strike and lay the one to the other, he intoned, "There's been another."

"From your presence here I had gathered as much. That confirmed by the slight asymmetry of your collar and the state of your shoes. Add to that the hour and . . ." I trailed off, leaning back into my own chair and reaching for my nearby pipe. "Surely the facets of this latest bloodshed are as common and unmarked as those others of your district."

"That's the problem, Mr. Holmes! It's clear as mud and reeks as much. My men and I are completely in the dark, and the public is starting to scream for our own necks. Your name came up. Given me by Inspector Lestrade."

There was no sense in hiding my own flash of surprised amusement. Far better he see that than the annoyance which often came from linking the inspector's name to mine. Lestrade was a good enough sort of man. He was even a passably adequate policeman at times. But if I were to be dragged out of my flat merely to watch several of the Yard's finest hem and haw over some dead-end crime of passion? No, I would not allow even Lestrade to bandy my name about so freely.

Still I had to, at the very least, hear Sir Charles through. Closing my eyes, I waved that he proceed with the details. A part of me wondered what Watson would think of it all now that my hand had been forced. Knowing him, he would be shrugging on his coat and taking out his little pen and pad rather than be left out of the action.

"Well, you see, we're now of the opinion that this whole thing began a month back, with the murder of Mrs. Martha Tabram. Found on the landing of the George's-buildings, top of George Yard on August 7th. Laid out on her back in a pool of blood, she was discovered by a lodger going out to work early in the morning."

"An overcast night with some small showers of rain. A new moon, and therefore as dark as could be conceived." I remembered the incident, remembered its peculiar lack of leads. "Stabbed thirty-nine times. Two suspects detained and later released."

"Mistaken identity in each case. And, besides, there were the character witnesses for both. Exemplary men."

"No doubt," I commented drily. "Pray continue."

"August 30th. Mary Ann Nichols is found slain in Buck's Row. 'Twas beginning of the last quarter and a partly cloudy night—so not as pitch as on the previous, Mr. Holmes. And a good rain storm the afternoon before so that we had more to work with. Victim was cut up like the other. Throat was slashed almost ear to ear—easy cause of death there. Her clothes had soaked up most of the blood, so much so that the first impression from the constable who found her was that she was merely a downed drunk. Three policemen in the area and nobody heard a sound, you see.

"But it was the post mortem examination that surprised us. The papers, as I'm sure you know, were none too circumspect in their reporting of the woman's further injuries. Abdomen and belly all hacked to bits. Some bruising on the face and throat. Strangulation therefore clearly the reason no one heard a thing."

"Who was it that performed the post mortem?"

"Dr. Llewellyn. His surgery is not more than three hundred yards from the site of the murder." Here Sir Charles gave the slight shudder of guilt for which I had been waiting. As I say, I had followed the reports in the papers with some degree of interest. "There was a small issue with that, I must admit. Two workers came by to strip and clean the body when the victim was left for a few moments. Honest mistake."

"But a terrible one. Something, some key fact, might have been missed by this, Commissioner. A hair; a lost button. A smudge of dirt or worse."

"I wholeheartedly agree, and there has been a dressing down of all involved. But it is about this morning's murder that I come to you in particular. Those that precede it merely indicate the pattern. Both in timing and in how little we have to go on. But this morning—it has points. It has points, Mr. Holmes. The first man on the scene, Inspector Joseph Chandler, immediately telegrammed the Yard."

And there the dropping of the name "Sherlock Holmes," I supposed. I refilled my pipe and waited.

"The woman—we're still working on getting her name—was laid out like the last. Found in the yard back of 29 Hanbury at just past six this morning. Throat sliced. Stomach opened up. And here's the ticket, Mr. Holmes. A leather apron was found in the yard by the fence. Wet. As though it had been washed of blood."

"And before you move against the owner of said leather apron, Lestrade thought it worth your while for me to take a look at the scene and evidence, yes?"

"In following the case, you'll have heard that we've a suspect."

I snorted, remembering the colourful descriptor in one of the Wednesday evening papers. The man who had caught the public's eye enjoyed a less than stellar reputation amongst his fellows. No less than fifty people had stepped forward to offer statements, from personal grievances to physical descriptions of the man who ran by the nickname of "Leather Apron" due to that article generally being a part of his daily costume. According to the press, nobody knew his name but that he moved in shadows on soundless feet, his eyes glittered wickedly, and his incessant grin repelled. While his name was yet a mystery, the police had, apparently, discovered his lodgings—conveniently empty of its inhabitant these past several days.

The Commissioner cleared his throat. "As you know, we are always careful lest we overlook something. The public wants to know why there's been no arrest. And after this morning's murder . . ."

At this my eyebrows raised of their own volition. "The woman. She's been taken to the mortuary for a post mortem?"

"Under strict instructions that the body is not to be touched until after both Doctor Phillips and yourself have made of it what you will. And I've left men blocking the yard of number 29. Crowds were beginning to gather, you understand."

Already I had found my feet and was reaching for my hat and coat. Ringing for Mrs. Hudson, I gave her notice of where the commissioner and I were heading, along with a directive that she pass word to Doctor Watson. His good sense often overrode my intractable ways, and though I did not yet believe the criminal actions in Whitechapel fell within my usual purview, there was something in the events that niggled at the back of my mind. A strange disquiet had seized my spirit, and I came away from Baker Street pondering the threads of uncustomary caution and concluding that if I were to be lured into this case, then Watson must come with me.

The commissioner and I turned our attentions upon a waking London. Neither of us found excuse to talk save to comment obliquely upon the weather. Autumn had sneaked into the air some time during the night, and a bright sun-washed sky met our eyes on the way to the waiting cab. For my part, I merely wondered how long it would be until the morning's freshness fully erased what evidence might be left in the dirt of my crime scene. No matter. The police had likely turned it into their parade ground by now.

At length, Commissioner Warren and I found the traffic slowing and the buildings on either side turning from smart to slapdash. Even arriving from the north, for three full blocks we witnessed an aimless crowd. Curiosity makes a holiday of tragedy, and one could feel the apprehension thickening the already pungent air of Spitalfields. At the market we disembarked, finding that our pace had slowed to the point of uselessness. It would not do for the papers to know more than us before the day was out. We proceeded on foot to 29 Hanbury where Warren's first man on the scene met with the commissioner and me.

"Inspector Joseph Chandler. Mr. Sherlock Holmes."

"The man who made the discovery, yes." I offered my hand and the policeman gave it two hard pumps.

"Happened in 'ere." Turning, he led us up and through the entrance of the house. Ducking into the narrow passageway and out of sight from meddling eyes, we fixed our attentions on the open door yawning into the yard beyond.

While the body had been taken off to the mortuary and some small disturbance of the dirt and stone had been necessary for that manoeuvre, I could almost believe that efforts had been made to preserve what marks might have been present upon discovery of the scene. Darting my eyes over the small yard, I read the prints as a lady might pore over the latest novel. All description and no plot, I could discern the edits of many a man and many a boot. Inwardly I sighed.

"She lay here?" I pointed.

"With her head almost at the steps, yes. Legs splayed wide and her skirts disarrayed—"

"And someone was here before you—not the murderer—who attended to her and raised the cry for help. Have you found the men who gave the alarm then? Questioned them?" Picking my way gingerly along the fence, I bent and indicated a set of divots and scuffs where someone had clearly knelt beside the body. "I perceive more than one attempt here at ascertaining whether the woman yet lived, and I doubt that any arrivals beyond yourself were mistaken as to the state of things."

"A Mr. John Davies discovered the body at six and ran for help. It was him who lowered her skirts. For decency. I, er, I grabbed some sacking to cover the woman. Again, it seemed wrong to have her lying thus, what with the crowd pressing and all. I took his statement."

"Thank you, Inspector," I murmured and then gestured to the detritus laid about the space. "And the rest of these items?"

"Left as found, sir. Only the body has been moved."

"And the leather apron." My eyes met his, and I pointed to the corner where a dripping pump further added to the damp of the ground.

Inspector Chandler flushed. "Yessir. In our excitement of finally having a concrete lead on the scoundrel . . ."

I did not listen to the rest of his explanation. Rather, I was intent on what else the ground had to tell me. "The money. That was left here by her feet? Along with"—eyeing the dirt sidelong, I squinted —"rings? Two rings, Inspector. Where have they gone off to?"

"No idea, sir. Perhaps robbery was the motive."

A small smile graced my lips. "It is certainly a thought, Inspector, though considering the economics of the surrounding, those coins would have been tempting as well. And at her head? This paper was there?"

"Just so. We left it for you to see."

I returned to the steps and leaned forward to pick it up. Part of an envelope, it contained a piece of paper wrapped 'round two pills.

"London, 28 Aug. 1888," I read the post office stamp aloud and peered at the writing scrawled across the front. An "M" and "Sp" were all that remained of any sort of address. On the reverse? The seal of the Sussex Regiment. "Medicine and an envelope of most specific origins, Inspector. If nothing else, it may show us who the unfortunate woman was."

"Or deliver us the man who done it. Military connexions would make the search easier."

Offering over the envelope and ignoring the policeman's quick assumptions, I again moved along the fence, taking out my lens and examining the length and breadth of it. No signs of entry or egress that way. Some blood spatter—as to be expected even were the woman to have been

15

rendered unconscious before having her throat slashed.

"What does it all mean, Mr. Holmes?"

I straightened and regarded the commissioner. "I have no doubt the coroner's report will note this latest victim was asphyxiated prior to the murderer drawing his knife over her throat. She was discovered dead, not dying, not crying out for help, and there are no clear signs in the yard of any sort of struggle. After bringing her down peacefully, our man slit her throat and then likely proceeded to attack the other portions of her body which show injury. He was in no hurry. As you see, he has taken the time to arrange her possessions just so. The leather apron is not his. The envelope is of some interest, as I said, if only in helping us determine the name of the victim and next of kin. The full duration of the attack—if the culprit, indeed, is the perpetrator of the previous murders and is as skilled as the papers have suggested—would have taken between five and twenty minutes depending on the extent of the woman's wounds. Our suspect would be bloodied but by how much I cannot say until we've had word from Doctor Phillips. Also, our killer would have left the way he came in."

Any further sharing of my conclusions was halted by a commotion down the hallway leading to number 29's front door. A change in its lighting, as well as a discordant shuffling and swearing, advertised a newcomer, and I could see both the inspector and commissioner tense.

"Impossible situation, I tell you. Absolutely outrageous!" The speaker gesticulated wildly as he came at us. Sparking and intelligent eyes sat betwixt wilful eyebrows and hawkish nose. The irate mouth positively trembled. All this was set amongst curly locks and bushy side whiskers and further framed off by the gentleman's well-cut suit and stovepipe hat.

"Ah, Doctor Phillips. We were just coming to see you."

"Then you'll go away disappointed," he huffed and turned his complaint to the commissioner. "Your PC off and went. And so they've done away with what evidence I might have worked, sir."

"I beg pardon?" Sir Charles appeared taken aback.

"The body's been stripped and washed. Before I could examine her as I ought. It's an outrage."

"The instructions were clear——"

"The instructions were ignored!"

"Gentlemen, I think it would be best if we had this discussion elsewhere. Doctor, perhaps you might be able to tell us what you've already concluded per your initial examination here?"

At last Doctor Phillips seemed to bow to my mollifying influence. He finished his complaint with a gruff, "Come along then," and led the way back out. The three of us followed meekly—two mortified policeman and I, somewhat embarrassed to be party to the parade of errors which plagued the investigation.

"A-ha!"

My triumphant exclamation caused my companions to jump.

"Points, Commissioner. And perhaps more instructive than someone's washing left along the fencing between back yards. A light, if you please, Inspector." Following my gaze, the man shone his lantern up into the brickwork lintel of the doorway. Scrawled in pale chalk the message ran:

. . .

Five. Fifteen more and then I give myself up.

Every man's blood ran cold at the sight, mine
included. My adrenaline hurried to catch it up. I
hardly knew I had drawn my glass out once more
and only distantly noted that Inspector Chandler's
light obligingly followed my motions.

"Is it he?"

"As I would doubt this to be the general motif of
interior decoration even in parts such as these, yes I
believe this the handiwork of our man." I leaned
close, sniffing at the writing and gingerly rubbing my
index finger along the edge of the last word. I
stepped back and considered. "We now can confirm
the handedness of our suspect. His general sense of
fair play—such as it is. And—hullo there."

I stopped short, eyes drawn downward to a small,
whitish cylindrical item upon the ground. The
rubbish had a friend. Two cigarette nubs. I picked
them up, almost dropping them a moment later. I
am uncertain as to whether my shock was displayed
for all. If so, no one made comment.

Tantamount to seeing the pale square of a baby's
bonnet lying at the bottom of a well, the terror that
it cast upon my mind was illogical and somehow
sickening. Two stubs said that the man had stayed
within this doorway far longer than it would have
taken for him to chalk his note. That or—and this I
thought the more probable of the scenarios—he had
saved his leavings for the express purpose of taunting
us further. It was a message, same as the words
scrawled on the wall above. The disquieting consid-

eration that I, in particular, was being toyed with, was made then quickly dropped, the action much like the recoiling of one's fingers from the reach of a snapping beast.

"Mr. Holmes?"

I shook myself out of my stupor and gave, what I am sure was, a wan smile. "Apologies, Inspector. Let us continue."

I let fall the two stubs, certain I had been wrong to attach any importance to such a trifle. We continued on towards the mortuary. What I learned there nearly put out of my mind the strange coincidence of the spent cigarettes. The Commissioner's brief summary in 221B proved a grave understatement. Doctor Phillips' findings were, by far, some of the most gruesome I had ever encountered. The man who had laid open 29 Hanbury's victim had not merely hacked and stabbed at her abdominal region. I learned that the woman's intestines had been lifted out of place and arranged with cruel deliberation, much as had the contents of her pockets. Worse still, the uterus had been surgically removed. Clean cuts, the murderer clearly possessed no small amount of anatomical knowledge. And nerve. The doctor believed the mutilations could have taken no less than a quarter hour and quite possibly longer.

We returned to the scene to question what witnesses the police had gathered. By now a queue had formed in spite of efforts to deter gawkers. An enterprising neighbour had taken it upon themself to profit from the tragedy. People were paying a penny to view the yard out back of number 29.

Mrs. Richardson, who lived above the ground floor shop, was irate. "Tell 'em there's nothing to see.

I've a business here. I've a home. And you, you leave my son alone. He's done no wrong."

This last came with a finger wagged at me, and I looked to Mr. Chandler.

"The apron is evidence against the man we're eager to capture, woman," Commissioner Warren stepped in to explain. "And so, if you claim the article belongs to your son? Well then, we must see it through."

I turned away from the scene and focussed on the other woman whom the police had questioned. Solid and matronly, her face carried both the wan paleness of a troubled mind and the sharp glint of determination. This was a witness with something to say and would say it to any who would listen. I decided to try her.

"You saw the man. Did you also see the woman?" Approaching, I began without preamble, startling her into candour.

She nodded and said, "I was walking westward to Spitalfields at five thirty when I saw a man and a woman standing up against the shutters of number 29. Her face I saw but the man's I could not, as he had his back to me. He was a little taller than the woman. Perhaps a half a foot, but then he wasn't standing straight."

"Did either appear intoxicated?"

"No, sir. Neither appeared the worse for drink. They were just . . . leaning. Talking. I didn't think anything of it. I didn't even have a good look at his face. Only hers."

"They were talking," I prompted. "About what?"

"I am not sure. I heard him say 'Will you?' and her respond with 'Yes,' but that's all I remember. I didn't attach any importance to it until I heard about

20

the murder and knew I might have seen the man that the woman was talking to, the man who done it."

"You've seen the victim then?" This surprised me.

"No, sir. But the timing—I remember the clock chiming. It couldn't have been anyone else."

"And the man's appearance?"

"Foreign. Maybe. And no older than forty. Again, I didn't get a look at his face. He didn't look like a worker, though, from his manner of dress. He looked like, what I should call, shabby-genteel. He had on a brown felt hat with a low crown and a long, dark-coloured coat."

When it appeared no further details were to follow, I smiled and gave the witness my thanks. I looked around to find the police had lost in the war against curiosity. Sir Charles and the rest were adrift in a growing crowd of onlookers. He caught my eye and sidled close, "Now you see what it is we're dealing with here."

I wanted to point out that, what we had in Hanbury Street at present, was not near what we were truly dealing with. But then he well knew the scope of the situation.

"Fifteen more and then I give myself up."

With little left to do there, I begged leave and promised I would consult with Inspector Lestrade as soon as I had a theory of any value. Returning home, I found that, in my absence, I had missed a visit from Watson. A spent cigarette marked the minutes he had waited before going on his way.

And there my traitorous brain betrayed me. The whole of the ghastly scene had replayed in my mind as I had ridden home, a shadowy figure occupying the role of the mysterious Whitechapel Murderer. Each time, I had found it harder and harder to get past the damning fact of the cigarette butts left beneath the chalked taunt to the police—to taunt me! And here was that same clue come home to Baker Street.

"Bradley, Oxford Street" had read the stamp upon the two stubs. So, too, read the remnant left behind in my apartment by my friend. This was what had so shocked me at Hanbury number 29. Cigarettes from Watson's tobacconist. At a murder scene.

The establishment itself lay not even one mile south of 221 Baker Street and had, of course, innumerable customers. Going there would produce nothing save frustration and the eventual sideways glance from both owner and patronage. And though my Watson was hardly the only man to patronize that shop, the evidence spoke to the class of man who had been in 29 Hanbury in the early hours of the morning.

We were looking for a gentleman wholly out of place in that street and yet someone who nobody noticed while everyone was looking for him. A person who would have had blood upon their hands and clothing. A butcher who ripped entrails from women and left them dead in gutters. A criminal who had, by his own claim, struck five times already and hoped for fifteen more. A man who had struck, seemingly, at random and yet also decided to make this case personal . . . for me.

By the time the evening *Star* shone its headlines upon the city, my own mind had sunk into a haze of tobacco and consternation. They, of course, had everything wrong, as the papers often do. But the overall effect remained stamped upon all of London's psyche, Baker Street's included:

HORROR UPON HORROR. WHITECHAPEL IS PANIC-STRICKEN AT ANOTHER FIENDISH CRIME. A FOURTH VICTIM OF THE MANIAC.

CHAPTER 2

"I have, for some time now, considered myself
hardened to what the criminal mind can
produce. But this, Watson . . . This is no ordi-
nary crime. You were right to warn me away from it,
I'll admit." Together he and I sat smoking compan-
ionably in my rooms at Baker Street. Not quite three
weeks had gone by since my sojourn to 29 Hanbury,
and we—that is to say, the police—were no closer to
finding anything resembling a solution to the case of
the Red Fiend.

It is not to say I had done nothing in the days
that had followed. I had visited each of the sites asso-
ciated with the Whitechapel Horror—not for any
fresh evidence they might offer, but, rather, in an
attempt to put myself in the place of our killer and
so better gauge his actions and movements. But that
mind stayed closed to me.

Watson would have said that a good thing but for
the fact of my not having seen my friend during that
protracted period. I had, indeed, begun to think him
ducking my various communiqués and invitations to

Baker Street. Terse excuses had been sent to 221. Or perhaps I had only read his notes in the light of my own frustrations on the case. It would not have been the first time I had fallen into the dumps of sulky annoyance.

"At least he came 'round to apologise."

"Who? Lestrade?" I indulged in a brief mirthless laugh. "Half explanation, half evasion of the mistakes his department has made in the case. I wouldn't venture to call that an apology. He ought to have excused himself for involving me at all if they were not going to listen to what I had to say."

"And still you fret, Holmes," Watson's correction came coloured by his usual depth of feeling.

"How could I not?" Being in no mood for such an exchange, I must admit I allowed my temper to best me. Knocking the remnants from my pipe into the cold ashes of the fire, I gained my feet to go pace by the window, my voice rising alongside. "Two suspects detained and released—neither of them matching in half what I profiled for our man. No, the police would rather pursue the useless lead perpetuated by rumour, racialism, and the terrible crime of a woman's having left her son's washing to dry along a fence-top! Everything I have said has been patently ignored. They have botched two post mortems through egregious miscommunication. And—"

Stopping, I drew a steadying breath and fixed my eye on my friend. "And women are dead. Five, he said. Five dead and fifteen more to come, if his threat is to be believed."

To his credit, Watson made no rejoinder. Rather, he let me come back around of my own accord. I sat and relit my pipe. "It's a dark business, Watson.

Deeper waters than you or I have yet waded. But of course you are right in that I cannot give it up, if but for the very fact of the murderer's message scrawled over that doorway in Hanbury."

In his quiet, affable, and utterly indispensable way, Watson leaned back in his chair and waved encouragement at me with his little note-book and pen. "The facts, Holmes. What do we know now— from the inquests, from the further investigations of the police, bungled though they have been."

"And in telling you, I will refresh for myself the pertinent facts, no doubt." I gave my friend a sly glance through heavy-lidded eyes. How often I have chanced to state that Watson learned little from me. Such a claim is shortsighted and ignores the human element of the science of deduction. I found myself reminded of how, in his ten months of marriage to our former client, I had sorely missed the dear doctor's easy encouragement. The lack of it in my life had had poor effect on my humour. "Very well. We now know the names of all three women who are rumoured to have been slain by the so-called Whitechapel Murderer. This leaves two unknown and unconsidered victims, if we are to take the chalked message at its word. Martha Tabram, Mary Ann Nichols, and Annie Chapman, the last of whose inquest ended this past Wednesday—"

"But not Emma Smith?"

I raised my eyebrows. I had not known Watson to be following the case as closely as that.

"In Emma Smith's case the victim was also her own witness, according to the inquest as reported in *The Times*. She had claimed that three men attacked her and that robbery had been the clear motive. And though her injuries were so grievous as to lead to her eventual death, they lack the distinctive flavour of these recent murders. No, the slight-of-hand required for the killer to have slipped off unknown in both Hanbury Street and George Yard indicates something more outré."

We suspended our recapitulation as the door opened and ushered in Mrs. Hudson. It would seem that I was not the only person in 221 Baker Street delighted to have Doctor Watson back for an afternoon. The woman forever expressed her affection through food and was heavily laden with the equipage of a substantial tea. With no word save for a warning glance to me, she left our apartment. The door clicked shut behind her, and I arose to go take my medicine in the form of food and drink. Watson took up his customary spot, and for a moment, all was as it had once been.

"And so the Yard's 'Leather Apron' is cleared of any charges, having availed himself of an unshakable alibi," Watson offered at length.

"John Pizer was located, questioned, and released. Along with a Mr. William Piggott, arrested for having upon him a bit of blood and some suspicious wounds. Him they could get no sense out of, and so he was released to an infirmary."

"Thus ends the short and useless parade of the Yard's suspects."

"None of whom closely resemble any witness description—thin as it is—nor my own conclusions of height and build based on the evidence found at number 29."

"And the letter? The one with the Sussex seal?"

"Again the police were determined to follow the wrong track. Seduced by the scent of yet another easy suspect, they followed the so-called pensioner,

Mr. Edward Stanley, with whom our victim had shared some intimacy. Whereas I followed the envelope to its more obvious source: the Royal Sussex regiment itself. I recruited Inspector Chandler for the task, and he spoke with the regiment's adjutant who explained that, the envelope not having been mailed from camp, excluded any of their own as a potential sender. Our unknown correspondent was either a soldier on leave or not a soldier at all. Our trail grew cold. More so when the inspector proved his mettle and visited area post offices where he was informed that the regimental stationary had been seen for sale all over as of late. Another dead-end. At least until one of Dark Annie's former lodge-mates came forward to explain, quite simply, that he'd seen her pick up the discarded bit of envelope off the mantle to use as a container for the medicine meant to treat her lung condition."

Watson shook his head. "So deucedly simple. That Inspector Chandler, he'll go far."

"Tell that to the coroner," I spoke into my teacup, recalling the none-too-kind commentary from the inquest.

"Well. I'm still holding out on the hope that the message left at the last scene was some sort of elaborate prank meant to put everyone on edge and cause all manner of mischief," Watson concluded. "We have had a quiet three weeks."

I smiled, shaking my head over my friend's dogged optimism. "A prank left in an out of the way space rather than above or next to the gruesomely conspicuous scene of the crime itself. No, Watson, it was a message meant for the police to find, the culprit knowing how they would comb over that entryway, puzzling over how it was he got in and out without being seen or heard. The question is not only who and why, but what. What is his game? What drives a man not only to brutal murder but to gloating in the afterward? What does he gain by telling us his next move?"

"Surely you have some theory then. The one of which the police have taken no heed."

At this, tepid water seemed to seize within my veins. I poured out my rationale on the case after but a moment's hesitation. I said, "Putting together what thin accounts we have from witnesses along with the physical evidence, our man is a reasonably intelligent, right-handed man who is inadequately disguising himself as one of sinister tendencies. He has a medical background. Is of medium to tall stature and possessed of fairly consequential strength of limb and nerve. His knowledge of the East End is adequate, if not a fair bit better than most—I doubt he is leaving the choice of location for his activities to fall fully on chance or the whim of his victims. Dressing well but not ostentatiously, he blends in easily with any crowd while also attracting the eye of the sort of women who've succumbed to his ploy. A long, dark coat handily conceals blood. A deerstalker cap and moustache—both noted by witnesses—help to hide his face. That said, he wishes for fame though he is, perhaps, unaware of it himself. Lastly, he is a consummate liar."

"Well!"

The look upon my face must have been positively forbidding, such was the reaction it elicited from my friend. I well knew that I was not often subject to fits of fancy and so took my outburst as further sign that this case was straining every nerve which I possessed. Oh, let Watson be right, I cried inwardly. Let it be over and done. Let us not hear of one more sensational ripping in the night.

Into that deafening silence intruded the downstairs bell. Importunate footsteps sounded a moment later on the stair. And bursting into the sanctity of our rooms came the familiar ferreted face of Inspector Lestrade of Scotland Yard. He said, "There's been a new development in the Ripper case."

"Not another murder?" Watson was on his feet.

"No. Mr. Holmes? What do you make of this?" Lestrade held in his shaking fingers a crumpled, stained envelope.

DEAR BOSS

CHAPTER 3

Accepting the item from Lestrade, I bade him sit while I made my brief examination. The envelope had passed through many hands before it had found its way into mine. Stains and creases covered the whole of it, but the address, penned in a strong hand and boastful red ink, could still be plainly discerned.

I read it aloud for the benefit of my companions as Watson poured a cup of tea for the inspector. "It is addressed to 'The Boss, Central News Office, London City.' Posted on the 27th. Just two days ago."

I shot a dark, questioning glance to Lestrade. His cup rattled into its saucer none too gently as he said, "They only gave it to us this morning. I came to you straight as I could. Lots of folks have needed to have eyes on it first, you see."

I removed the short missive from within the weathered envelope and cast a quick eye over its contents. What I found had me blindly seeking for the chair behind me.

"Holmes! Dear God, man. What is it?" Watson started to his feet, and I waved him off.

With a mouth gone dry, I read the following, "It says:

25 Sept. 1888.
  Dear Boss,

I keep on hearing the police have caught me but they wont fix me just yet. I have laughed when they look so clever and talk about being on the right track. That joke about Leather Apron gave me real fits. I am down on whores and I shant quit ripping them till I do get buckled. Grand work the last job was. I gave the lady no time to squeal. How can they catch me now. I love my work and want to start again. You will soon hear of me with my funny little games. I saved some of the proper red stuff in a ginger beer bottle over the last job to write with but it went thick like glue and I cant use it. Red ink is fit enough I hope ha. ha. The next job I do I shall clip the ladys ears off and send to the police officers just for jolly wouldnt you. Keep this letter back till I do a bit more work, then give it out straight. My knife's so nice and sharp I want to get to work right away if I get a chance. Good Luck.
  Yours truly
  Jack the Ripper

Dont mind me giving the trade name

. . .

Wasnt good enough to post this before I got all the red ink off my hands curse it. No luck yet. They say I'm a doctor now. ha ha"

For a long moment after nobody moved. Nobody spoke. And then,

"Why, he's toying with us!"

"But is it real, Mr. Holmes?"

Watson and Lestrade each passed judgment upon the whole of it. As for me, I remained seated in my chair and merely stared at the letter in my hand. Not examining, just . . . looking. Thinking. Fearing.

At length I rose and went over to my desk. Reaching for my strong lens, I held the letter up to the light, examining both front and back. I made my conclusions and then spoke, "Four days ago, a man wrote this letter and, after some consideration, decided to post it. That he sent it to the Central News Agency rather than, say, *The Times* or Scotland Yard, is interesting. A paper might not have been able to resist the urge to publish it straight off, and he seeks to control the narrative. Note how he has asked that the recipient keep this letter back for a while longer which, unfortunately, appears to be what the agency did before eventually forwarding it on to the Yard as they ought to have from the first. Far better for him to stew, to anticipate and plan his next attack —for attack again he most certainly will, and not merely for having promised it within these pages.

"The paper itself is unremarkable. You can find its like in any shop in town. Same too, the ink and envelope. His pen is in very good condition. See here how even his emphatic underlining came through strong and unscratched in spite of the emotional force it carries. The back of the letter—it would appear that our man was careless enough to have had another paper beneath it while he penned his inflammatory missive, though discovering what it might have been is of needle and hayfield proportions.

"It is a steady hand, a confident hand, who has penned this threat. It is, moreover, a right-handed script. See how at the end where he has concluded and signed his name that the strokes change and the lines themselves slope gently upwards? Here he is at his most comfortable. The writing style overall shows a fair degree of self-control. This trait has been evidenced already in the locations of the killings, if not in the manner. He is smart and he is careful. He could well be the man next door, your neighbour or mine. His only master is drama in which he cannot help but indulge. I have hopes that this will prove his undoing."

The letter I let fall upon my desk, and I rested my chin upon my fingers to think.

Lestrade spoke up. "That ears comment. He's thumbing his nose at us again, Mr. Holmes."

"A threat, Lestrade, yes. It is like the message chalked upon the wall. Theatrics meant to stir our souls and bring to mind greater horrors still to come. He writes with red ink but alludes to blood. The sort of man who knows how to dissect a woman as Jack has would, too, be learned enough to know that he could not have saved the"—I consulted the letter —" 'Proper red stuff' in a beer bottle for later use. Our man is a master at painting with imagination."

"But the Croydon business." Lestrade refused to be mollified. "How the devil would he know to make such a jibe? That was six years ago, and I made certain the details of the case did not make the papers."

I looked to Watson. He had made no comment during the heated exchange and had, instead, seemed to turn his attentions inward. He noticed my scrutiny and tried to rouse himself. "Croydon business. Yes. I'm sorry, but I don't recall the particulars of that incident."

Lestrade gawked. "You were with us on that case, man. The ears? Erroneously sent in a cardboard box to Miss Cushing of Cross Street, Croydon rather than to her sister. We caught our man from the type of twine used to close the packet."

Watson squirmed uncomfortably in his chair. "Well, yes, well, my notes, you see . . ."

"We are three of, perhaps, seven people in all of England who know of the case," Lestrade said. "And I—"

"We can all agree on one thing, Lestrade. This so-called Jack the Ripper will strike again, and that is the problem which attracts our attention today." I drew his eye back upon our present case even as I took up the letter again.

He scowled. "And undoubtedly this Jack will not be so convenient as to provide us with a particular knot you can trace, Mr. Holmes. Well, we have a plan for him. As of this morning, the Yard has taken charge of the local forces, and we have engaged the services of every man that is practical. Our plan is to position them about every place most likely for the murderer to attack in the coming days. Next to none will be uniformed, and they're to dine, drink, and smoke to their hearts' happiness while on this special duty. The aim is to blend in with the local populace and not let the Ripper know how tight our net is upon him."

"How marvellous!" Watson beamed.

I grunted and made to rise. "Lestrade, I should very much like to see—nay, to participate in—your ecumenical approach to policing Whitechapel this evening. Watson and I both, if I may be so bold as to volunteer him. You don't mind coming along with me for one of my 'pretty little problems' even though you've been domesticated, Doctor?"

"Not at all, Holmes." He rose to take his leave. "I will have to go along home for a brief time this afternoon, however, so as not to unduly distress Mary."

"Of course, of course." I waved a distracted hand his way. My eyes had re-discovered the letter on my desk and were telegraphing to my mind several new possibilities. Lestrade cleared his throat. I turned to the two men gracing my sitting room and gave them a good looking over. "Lestrade, will you be partaking in the ruse? Good. Whatever instructions you're providing to your men I am certain you can emulate. But Watson? Ah, never mind."

Flashing a wan smile, I let my query die unasked. There would be time enough in the afternoon to work on the doctor's transformation. Again that strange quaver had risen in my chest as I looked to my friend, and I shrank instinctively from having him make a promise he was sure to break by evening's end. Something in his manner, a shadow under the mask of his smile, had gained the attentions of my more clinical self.

I longed to return to the Ripper's letter. But, alas, Lestrade's impatience was growing marked. Reluctantly I handed over the evidence and saw him out. I then turned to Watson, determined now to not fall to the emotional pitfall which had almost snagged me moments before. "Come 'round at, say, seven? I am certain I could entice Mrs. Hudson to prepare a supper for two. And as for dress, I can come up with something suitable for both of us amongst my rags, but be sure to wear some inconspicuous shoes. Surely your wife has a pair of yours that she despises. Wear those."

Both visitors were scarcely out the door when I, too, made exit from 221B. Flying down the stairs, I passed a startled Mrs. Hudson, and though she was, by now, used to my quirks of practice, she still managed to call out a scolding, "Mr. Holmes!" after my retreating form. For my hasty hands were rearranging vest and shirt, pulling hair and pasting on a set of false 'brows. A tattered coat and none-too-straight cane completed the picture, and I was off in hot pursuit of my quarry.

Luck was on my side, and Watson never turned around to ascertain that he had a pursuer. And why should he? He had just left the house of a friend. This observation gave me a pang, for it spoke on the side of innocence and against my own suspicions.

Ah! But there! The doctor had not gone far when he turned his steps, hurrying into a telegraph office. I moved to follow. Unfortunately, contrary to every logical action, Watson came straight out of the building within moments. We nearly collided, in fact, and it was only through the utmost care on my part that I did not give up the game and expose myself to my friend.

"Good day, sir." With a distracted tip of the hat, he sidestepped me neatly on the path, and so I was able to see more of his expression and mood. He seemed rattled, his cheeks pale and eyes harbouring a wildness of spirit that did not belong within my friend's face. My antennae were incensed. Surely Watson would not have had time to send anything. Faced with no other choice but to continue on my own trajectory, I muttered a gruff greeting and ducked in the doorway.

Once inside, I fumbled about for an objective of my own. A solution presented itself. A telegraph form lay upon the ground, and I bent to retrieve it.

"It would appear that the gentleman has dropped this," I began, offering it out to the man at the counter. My sharp eyes raked over the partially-filled form.

"Thank you, sir. The man had, in fact, decided against sending his note in the end. The paper is of no importance whatsoever." The hard gaze which I received informed me that my impertinent assistance in recovering the dropped item was unwelcome and that I ought to state my own business there.

Scowling to better match my role's persona, I muttered something about needing to send a telegram—of course—and proceeded to hunt about my shabby pockets for the appropriate coin. As one might guess, I had none and so had to move along my rickety way and back into the street.

Ducking back 'round the corner, I breathed a quick sigh of relief, and returning home, I replayed in my mind the image of the discarded telegram form. The paper's addressee had been one "John H. Watson of 221B Baker Street" and the woefully incomplete message had read "Urgent—" and nothing else.

Why on earth would Watson consider sending himself a telegram? Why would he have it sent care of 221B, he who had scarce crossed its doorway these past ten months? What had he intended the message to say? And what would have caused him to change his mind so abruptly?

Several explanations shouldered forward. None were satisfactory in illuminating for me what weighed so strangely upon my friend's mind. For I had read Watson's face while Lestrade had talked. He remembered the Cushing case, that was certain. Why had he claimed the opposite?

I could follow him home. I could ask him outright. That, or I could wait and allow my friend to come 'round to the truth of it on his own. Assuredly the explanation was both logical and mundane. Or I could return home and steep my brains in the strongest shag tobacco I had in my possession. This last was the solution I adopted in the end.

TO CATCH THE DEVIL

CHAPTER 4

Emerging from my cloud of smoke two hours later in order to see to my own disguise for the evening and peruse the correspondence left for me by my ever patient landlady, I chanced upon a telegraph. It was from Watson.

WILL NOT MAKE IT THIS EVENING STOP HAVE BEEN CALLED AWAY TO A PATIENT STOP MAY COME BY TOMORROW STOP GOOD LUCK JOHN WATSON

The irony of it all was not lost on me. But it left me with a dilemma. I had promised myself to Lestrade for the evening. In all likelihood, we might align to prevent a murder. However, Watson's behaviour disturbed me. More than I cared to admit. For all that I had observed my friend firsthand, had pulled together the smattering of marks against him and dismissed them as folly and the product of a harried mind, my suspicions had been roused and were not easily put down.

Over and over I had turned the problem, asking myself whether it was I, through my paranoia and compulsive retracing of fact, who ought to fall under watchful scrutiny rather than my friend. The picture drawn by the evidence, however, was too stark to ignore. It was only my own reluctant thrashing about which had, so far, bought my silence on the matter. The police required a lead. They had next to nothing.

But didn't I, also?

I considered again the cigarette stubs found at 29 Hanbury. A trifle and, as I had already admitted, hardly damning of anyone who patronized that particular tobacconist. Similarly over-broad was the killer's height and build based on the evidence of the scenes. In a city five and a half million strong, such paltry limitations left nearly a million and a half men for consideration. But add in the Ripper's clear intelligence—consider, for example, his thin attempts in disguising his handedness and advertising for us pointedly poor grammar in his letter to the press—alongside his anatomical proficiency, and the picture of a man greatly resembling John Watson remained in focus.

That was only if I weighed the physical evidence.

In his emotional makeup, my dearest friend could be no closer to this dread Ripper than the sun to the moon. And yet . . . In the past ten months he had undergone a marked domestic change. He had left behind the rough and tumble of our work for a quiet hearth and respectable practice. I believed I knew John well enough to know that he would greatly miss our regular feats of derring-do and would find other ways to inject some small excitements into his life, much as I occasionally partook of recreational stimulants for my brain when my own work fell to drudgery.

Watson's little experiment in setting down some

of my more extraordinary cases had proven a double-edged blade. For both of us. Since his rather minor success in last year's *Beeton's Christmas Annual*, where the public was treated to the rather colourfully embellished tale of *A Study in Scarlet*, he had grown rather singularly minded in his pursuit of publication. There was talk of a formal novel and, perhaps, a serialized collection. While Watson had not made time to visit me of late, he had taken it upon himself to send me the occasional sketch of this or that case for my "approval"—or whatever sense of awe and accolade he felt he needed from me on his efforts. I had, generally, returned the packets of prose unthumbed and accompanied by the thinnest of notes. He might find enjoyment in such lurid undertakings as entertaining the groaning masses. Whereas, after *Beeton's*, I was now treated to a regular procession of curiosity seekers outside my home and increasingly onerous pleas for assistance in the forms of letters, telegrams and even—shudder—one telephone call that had gone to Mrs. Hudson rather than myself.

The temporary hitch in our relationship, one already stretched under his engagement and then marriage to Miss Mary Morstan, had grown into a great divide. But even under all that, Dr. John H. Watson, so far as I could tell, had not been acting like himself of late. He was furtive. Distracted. Almost sharp but not so much as to draw me out and force confrontation on my part.

Lastly: the letter. That damned letter. I could overlook a chalked message on a wall. After *Beeton's*, any deplorable could have got into his head the grand notion of leaving a cryptic threat at a crime scene. One might even excuse the pointed jibe at me through the cigarettes—though to come upon the knowledge of Watson's tobacconist and employ it was to know as much about the doctor as about myself.

But this Jack the Ripper character threatening to send the victim's ears to the police? It went beyond taunt. Outside of Scotland Yard, few people knew of the case Lestrade had brought to Watson and me in the early days of our partnership. It was an incident which John had come to reference more than a few times over our several years together. There the Ripper's threat had been carried out. A cardboard box containing two human ears had been sent to an unsuspecting woman. Macabre even by my standards. Such warped ideas did not often trip through the human psyche.

And I did not believe in coincidences.

Too, I had once told the doctor that I made no exceptions. Did I yet believe that to be true?

"Eliminate the impossible," I muttered.

But which was Watson's potential guilt: impossible? Or improbable? On this my mind and heart stood at odds. Evidence was such that his activities, at the very least, warranted a closer look. In the dire circumstances of this series of murders, were he anyone else—were I anyone else—he would have been subjected to some rather pointed questions. Either at the offices of the Metropolitan Police or here within 221b. Instead I had chosen the quiet route in the satisfaction of my suspicious mind and found yet another mystery on the steps of the telegraph office down the street. Lestrade would be furious if he knew. Incredulous, too. He might even indulge in a laugh at my expense. But the police detective would be furious all the same.

Well, even I was furious at myself for having impulsively discarded the importance of those cigarette butts. For if our case were to take any decided turn upon the advent of the Ripper's next move, should new evidence come to light and require the detritus from Bradley's of Oxford Street to hang a man—

The chiming of the hall clock stirred me from my malaise. Six o'clock. It was high time I readied myself for the night ahead. Crossing into the next room, I dove into my closet of miscellany. My disguise from earlier in the day would do me no good. I needed a touch more vulgarity. And if Watson should fall within our path tonight . . .

"No. Watson is with his patient, Sherlock," through clenched teeth I rebuked myself. The errant thought continued on its own, however. If Watson were to somehow unexpectedly make appearance this night, it would be best if I look nothing like how I had when I followed him to the telegraph office but hours before.

Within the hour, the ever-suffering Mrs. Hudson let out of her back door the seediest, most down on his luck chap that had ever graced the polished floors of 221. Ten minutes prior to that, she had sent on his way one small boy who had loitered by the front step chatting with the gentleman who lived in the rooms above. Watson's comings and goings would now be reported to me without my direct involvement.

Clutching grimy cap within my filthy and stained fingers, I found that I had ever so much trouble hailing any sort of cab. In the end, I secured for myself a dreary hansom to take me onward to Commercial Street. I was to meet with Lestrade at

Ten Bells but chose to disembark a good seven blocks early so that I might better insert myself into the locale and relieve my suspicious driver back where he could do my disguise no mischief through a pointed comment or action. Whistling tunelessly through my chapped lips and allowing my tongue to familiarize itself with its new cracked and chipped enamelled companions, I grinned into the cloudy, rain-heavy skies.

Freedom. Freedom and a deliciously lax morality, if only for a few fleeting hours. I wondered how Lestrade's men were getting on. I pondered Watson's whereabouts and again considered the curiosity of his aborted telegram to himself in light of his having sent me one in the end. A thin ruse which he thought better of the moment he went to enact it? Absurd. Suspicious. I put it out of my mind. And in its place slid the Ripper's knife. Wicked and gleaming in the darkness of my fears, I could see the weapon and the hand that held it. Was he, too, out on an evening such as this? Was this the night he would meet his end? Might I put a stop to his butchery?

A gush of freshening wind burst upon my upturned face. It was swiftly followed by the most inconsiderate of downpours. My outer garments were soaked through in seconds, and I dashed for the nearest doorway alongside the other foot traffic. Stamping and swearing, my temporary comrades and I sheltered from the rain. I was going to be late for my appointment with Lestrade. Inwardly I blessed the greasy substance that I had used upon my face and hands to dirty my features. The stuff was impervious to the rainfall. I extended my thanks to the storm itself for, if anything, the weather was a godsend as it rendered the night as inhospitable to murder as it did nigh on everything else.

The shower was a short one. With wan smiles, my little knot of companions broke apart, each going his own way. My battered coat and hat fairly steamed, and the clouds which had loosed down upon London now huddled close in an imitation of fog. I hurried my steps.

The pub stood on the corner ahead, one bright spot in a dreary darkness. A group of men gathered at the door. Policemen, all of them. I pushed my way past, seeking Lestrade. I had a beer in hand before I found the table at which he waited. Smiling, I ventured forward. At least he did not look like the Law. Seedy jacket, greasy hair, stained pants, and ruined shoes, it made a good picture, and I had to admit that I was rather impressed. But he was not drinking. Doubling back, I secured a second beer.

I was at least rewarded by the compliment of Lestrade not seeing through my disguise as I had his. Scowling, the man nearly refused my company until a whispered word from me gave the game away to him.

"Holmes!" He could not keep his bitten exclamation entirely hushed, but he tried. I smiled and simply brought my beer to my lips.

Casting my eyes about the room, I offered comment, "Either you've too many men at your disposal or you need to have them knot about in other places. The fellows at the door? Easily marked as plainclothes officers. They need to be drinking, Lestrade. Or at least pretending to."

I gave a pointed glance to Lestrade's untouched beer. He ceded my point, saying, "I told them all to bugger off to the dark places, the out of the way spots. But that rain got 'em, and they all came back. Smoke. Talk. Loiter, I told them. Only thing they're not allowed to do is go whoring."

I chuckled into my glass. "They'll scatter once they're bored. And I doubt that our man will strike before the wee hours of the morning."

"And why's that, Mr. Holmes?" Lestrade's sly face challenged me, and I flinched at this second use of my name. The inspector's disguise only went cloth-deep. Not that I was being much better at present. So few of the pub's patrons were locals, what with the sudden police presence.

I leaned in. "The pattern, Lestrade. This is a man who requires two basic elements to foment opportunity. Location and a willing victim."

"I seriously doubt that—!" Incensed, Lestrade forgot to keep his voice lowered for one harrowing moment but corrected himself swiftly. "I seriously doubt that these women are allowing themselves to be led to slaughter."

I clenched my jaw to the interruption. "Both pieces of the killer's puzzle are not often laid together until the waning hours of the night. Too much traffic in this district. Too many folks awake— particularly on a Saturday evening. And until they find themselves without their doss, he has not an easy and desperate victim willing to do immoral acts in secluded points."

"Apologies." Lestrade covered his error with a hasty draught of his pint. "It's just this damned business. It has me all on ends, Holmes."

"And I, Lestrade. And I." I drained my cup and slapped the table. "How about we walk about the neighbourhood."

"Do a bit of loitering ourselves." Lestrade's grin

served to further thin his sallow face. For all that it was a dangerous game—with ourselves, for once, not the likely target of violence—the inspector enjoyed himself. All at once, I felt a sort of strange kinship to the man. Perhaps all men who are stripped down to their bare essentials and left with nothing save for a gnawing fear feel as much. In any event, I was glad for his companionship as we left the Bells.

"Today hath this prophecy been fulfilled in your ears." Lestrade looked about the empty street in surprise.

"Come. Let us find our own out of the way locale in which to while away our night. I, for one, would be interested in seeing the various places where our Ripper has come calling in these past weeks. Perhaps his haunting ground holds meaning for him that we, ourselves, may discern. 'Den Teufel halte, wer ihn hält. Er wird ihn nicht so bald zum zweiten Male fangen.' "

I met Lestrade's scripture with the secular and moved off into the night. The phrase was as out of place in my character's mouth as it was in this sorry street.

Never mind that we had yet to catch the devil in the first place.

THE CRY OF "MURDER!"

CHAPTER 5

F aust.

Did that make me the devil's friend?

Setting off at a brisk pace up Commercial Street, Lestrade and I left behind any interested onlookers to our antics. I spotted three of his plain-clothesed officers in the short block and a half north. Rounding the corner onto Hanbury, we slowed. The windows of number 29 were shuttered and dark, but I could see a glimmer of light in one of the upper rooms.

" 'Ere now. Move along'n." A constable's light flicked our way as we lingered near the doorway. What happened next left me thoroughly astonished.

"Hurrah for the pot and the bottle!
      Hurrah for a drain on the sly,
      I mean now to well wet my throttle,
      And live like a cock till I die!

· · ·

"I've been selling the clock and the table,
 I've sold the old tub and the—
 I've sold the old tub and the—"

Here Lestrade stopped his raucous singing, seemingly stuck on the next word. Stumbling forward, he flung his arm about the constable, and I saw him get a word into the man's ear. Drunkenly grinning, the inspector leaned back and gestured to me.

Drawing a lungful of air I bellowed, "Pail!"

"Ah!" Lestrade's staggering cry of recognition was one for the music halls. "Pail!"

With a shake of his head, the constable flicked his light elsewhere and went on his way, and arm in arm, Lestrade and I strode off down the street singing our impromptu duet.

"I've been selling the clock and the table,
 I've sold the old tub and the pail.
 And this very life, if I'm able,
 I'll walk off the bed without fail.

"Hurrah for the pot and the bottle!
 Hurrah for a drain on the sly,
 I mean now to well wet my throttle,
 And live like a cock till I die!"

We made it to the street's end and around the next corner onto Baker's Row without further interruption. There Lestrade fixed me an admiring grin, and

I answered it with the same, adding, "You have unsounded depths, Inspector."

"Not one word to anyone on this, Holmes. Not a one, leastways to your sometime herald who likes to put your work into words and sell them to the magazines." Inwardly I thrilled at the oblique mention of Watson's literary endeavours. For it touched too close upon my fears for him. But in the darkness I could see Lestrade still smiling from ear to ear.

Our walk along Baker's Row was a short one, and turning onto the broad street of Dunward sobered us up. For here we now faced the scene of the second of the Ripper's murders. At this the skies opened up once more, a fitting gesture of lamentation from the heavens. Together, the inspector and I dashed for shelter.

"And no one heard a thing." Lestrade shook his head, his eyes fixed on the site of Mary Ann Nichols' death as we waited out the downpour. "Men at work all around. 'S a shame." I could have sworn I saw a tear in the eye of the work-hardened man of law, but perhaps it was an errant raindrop.

The rain continued to fall, isolating us each within our separate thoughts though we stood elbow to elbow within the same door. At length Lestrade took out a cigarette case. The silver flashed in the dim light, and I was reminded again of how flimsy the inspector's disguise was. A scratch of the match and sharp flare of phosphorus, and our little alcove soon bloomed in smoke. At his offer, I partook, nodding my thanks.

Lestrade stared at the spent match in his hand, rolling it between his fingers as he asked, "Do you recall that curious case we had back in March of '78?"

"The matchstick poisonings. An entire family murdered by the contents of one box of matches. Trebletary, I believe the name was, though I would have to consult my files to be certain."

"Clever thing, that. A murderer scraping match heads for his weapon so as to avoid the poison register and therefore escape detection. You lived in Montague Street then."

"And you hated my methods."

"Questioned them," he corrected, flashing me a smile.

"And now?" This was for my vanity, I will freely admit.

"I believe you are our only hope in this current business, Holmes. You who see what is darkness to the rest of us." He paused before continuing, "Having worked with you often, I know that you dearly love keeping much to yourself until your theories are provable. And, like the man we're seeking, you're not above a bit of the dramatic to stroke your ego. He plays your game, this Ripper. The letter. The message. It's a case designed to your specifications."

I turned to him. "What, pray tell, are you saying, Lestrade?"

Steadfast, he regarded me. "Nothing save for this: find this murderer, Holmes. Put a stop to this Jack the Ripper lest others spring up in his wake."

I looked away, my jaw tightening with my efforts to not say something rash. I flicked my spent cigarette into the darkness and leaned out of the doorway. The rain had ceased. We moved on, retracing our path to Baker's Row and turning south upon it to Whitechapel Road.

Here within that massive and wide thoroughfare

the traffic still slogged fitfully on. And in spite of the foul weather, we were not the only pedestrians present. Onward we journeyed, half a dozen or so blocks west until we ducked into the long narrow alleyway of George Yard via a covered archway.

"Hsst." My restraining hand upon Lestrade's arm brought him back close beside me in the shadows. Two whispering figures moved in the dark before us. A man and a woman. Their purpose became clear a moment later when the shorter of the two hitched up her skirts and bent over against the wall.

Both I and my companion tensed, ready should we be needed, but I had already dismissed the man as being our Jack. I found it unlikely that the killer would have grown nearly a foot in height over the last few weeks. Though myself no stranger to the art of disguise, such an alteration in stature on the part of our murderer would be impractical for his work and not at all in keeping with the sort of man given to advertising his next actions to the press.

The couple finished their act without incident. Lestrade and I backed out into Whitechapel long enough for the two paramours to depart via a more discreet exit.

"Like a rabbit warren." I noted no less than six points of egress from the narrow passage. And to think there were two or three such places upon every block and for miles on end. Even posting policemen every thirty feet throughout the whole of the East End would likely yield an imperfect barrier to trouble.

"Come, Holmes. Let us return to the main road."

Peering through archways into empty yards, we

picked our way to the north end of the street. We came out upon Wentworth and turned left, intent on returning to Commercial Street so as to find our way back up to Ten Bells.

We had taken no more than a dozen steps when:

"Murder! Police!"

Various shouts met our ears. Both Lestrade and I whirled around. My hand went to my right coat pocket wherein rode my pistol. The shrill shriek of a police whistle sounded an instant later. The cry was taken up, and the air filled with the discordant shouts of panic, London howling like a pack of mournful dogs. It chilled the blood yet quickened the pulse.

"There!" I pointed, and we followed the racing policemen. Our legs churned beneath us. The vast intersection of Whitechapel flew by in a blur. Onward we ran. By now, Lestrade had made clear his rank to a PC whom we passed. A small entourage of officials cleared our way through the gathering, anguished crowd.

"Down th' next block." A man within our escort pointed, and we turned right into Berner Street.

"Spread out. See that no man is left unquestioned who seems wrong," Lestrade bellowed. The command scattered the police presence.

And I? I entered the lonely and darkened gateway of the yard where the Ripper's latest victim lay.

ONE

CHAPTER 6

The body lay close by the wall. Several police lanterns had been left to illuminate the grisly sight. The light threw monstrous shadows upon the nearby brickwork and cast a sheen upon the spilt blood.

The woman's face was towards the wall, and her left arm lay outstretched. From six feet distant I could see that she had something clutched tight within her hand. Her legs were drawn up, and her skirts were hitched 'round her waist. Gentlemanly instinct fought with professional responsibility, and I clenched my fingers against the desire to protect her dignity from prying eyes. I turned away, concentrating on the yard itself.

The rain-moistened ground had done its best to preserve for me its story. There the tell-tale marks of a skittish pony and a cart that had to be backed laboriously out of the gate in the midst of a gathering crowd. Here the urgent and anxious footprints of the first to arrive at the scene, the toes having drilled further into the dirt than the heels. Running steps, they'd come and gone only to bring more back with them.

Crouching in the corner, I placed myself within the moment and watched the ghosts of first labourer, then members of the local Club, and finally the PC enter and leave the scene. Satisfied at the order of events but dismayed that, even with the rain, there had been enough activity in the yard to obliterate any obvious traces of our murderer, I approached the body.

"Inspector?" My call brought Lestrade back to my side. He had commandeered a light and now shone it over the woman's still form.

"Good God, Holmes." He turned away from the sight. I felt my own sympathies rise alongside. But, far from forcing an aversion of my gaze, the emotional swell acted as catalyst to my discernment. The night fell away. The corpse became a mere collection of data. Having spent its emotional coin, my mental state cleared. My knife's point of logic cut through the extraneous of horror and empathy.

Here was the killer. I could see him pulling at the victim's checked silk scarf, bringing her into his power before she could put up anything resembling a fight. Laying her down, he further robbed her of breath and then drew his weapon from left to right across the woman's throat. The skirts pushed up, the next wounds ready in his mind and then . . . A sound? Some disturbance in the street that set him to fleeing before he could complete his heinous ritual? I cocked my head, hearing the cart and horse approach. At that, the Ripper fled into the night.

Laying with my cheek close by the pavement, I flicked the policeman's light over the ground at the woman's side. A compressed rectangle met with a corner of the spilt blood, and I whistled my low exclamation of interest, peering closer and gently touching the disturbed dirt. Some object had been set there while the Ripper did his work. I rose and looked back down to the victim's face. "She still has her ears, Jack."

Reaching, I felt for the paper packet that lay clenched in the woman's hand. The lozenges within broke apart as I freed the small object from her stiffening fingers. Breath fresheners. No doubt then as to the occupation which had brought her into this deserted corner.

I rose to my feet and looked for Lestrade. Together we made another circuit of the yard while the officers on the scene supervised the moving of the body to the mortuary.

"Another labyrinth of options for our man," the inspector muttered, flashing his light into various corners.

"But what aided his escape also proved an added risk to his activities. This location is quite public. I even believe that he was chased off before he could quite finish his work."

"She looks well enough finished, Mr. Holmes."

To that I had nothing to say.

We returned to where the PC waited with several witnesses.

"Mr. Holmes, Inspector Lestrade, this is Mr. Louis Diemshutz."

The nervous man kept darting his eyes to the bloody pool by the wall. I moved to block his view. Mr. Diemshutz visibly relaxed after that small courtesy.

"I found her. Just like that. Thought it my wife at first. Panic, I suppose. I ran right into the Club to—"

"If we could have it from the beginning, Mr. Diemshutz," I prompted.

"It's like this then. I was coming back from a long day at Westow Hill. I sell jewellery, Inspector. A-and I—"

Again his eyes sneaked around my shoulder to peer at where the body had lain.

"My poor horse wouldn't move forward," came his broken whisper. "I tried to move on and ended up jumping down from my barrow to see what was what. Saw something lying there. Well, I thought it a woman lying dead or drunk. Took two matches for me to have the light to see her by. My wife, she works in the Club, you see, and all I could think about was her. So I ran in, grabbed a candle and came back out with two others of the members."

"And did you disturb the body at all, Mr. Diemshutz?"

Wide-eyed, he shook his head at Lestrade. "No, sir. In the candle's light we could all see the blood and so took up the cry for the police."

"Thank you, Mr. Diemshutz. You had best go inside and see to your wife." I turned to Lestrade saying, "I would also like to speak to the first officers on the scene. That and any other persons of interest that might have been detained within the last hour."

At this a man stepped forward. "Police Constable William Smith, sir. My beat takes me past Berner Street, and I can say that not a sound, not a scream, was heard. And I believe I saw the man."

"Oh?" Lestrade sidled close to listen. "Are you certain?"

"I saw the deceased after the crowds had come to gather in the entry of the yard here. It was the same woman that I saw on Berner not a half an hour before."

"A half an hour," I interjected.

"Yes sir. My beat takes about that long to bring me back around." He slid his eyes to Lestrade.

"And the man?" I redirected his attentions back onto me.

"I would gauge him to be around 28 years of age. He wore a felt deerstalker's hat, dark clothes, and a cutaway coat. He was a few inches taller than the woman, maybe five foot seven."

"Had he any whiskers?" Lestrade had interjected himself again.

"No, sir. But he was carrying some sort of parcel."

"A parcel?"

"Yes. Largish and wrapped in newspaper. Maybe a foot and a half long and six inches high."

"So not some small, easily pocketed trinket," I noted.

"He would have been seen carrying it while he fled, yes," the man followed my meaning. "That or he abandoned it somewhere in the neighbourhood."

At this Lestrade inclined his head to the waiting police officers and added Smith's mysterious package to the list of suspicious items for the evening. Inwardly I rolled my eyes. As much as I had harboured brief hopes at the mention of the news-paper-wrapped item, the facts simply did not fit. A gap of thirty minutes or so—this confirmed by the timing of Diemshutz's approach upon the scene—made it highly unlikely that PC Smith had seen our Jack.

In turns, others stepped forward to make their statements, some less eager for having been forcibly detained by the police. In fact, the entirety of the adjacent Club had been kept close at hand until a full search could be completed. This proved handy when our last witness came forth to tell his tale.

A broad-faced, pleasant looking man with a full chin of dark whiskers stepped forward at the PC's urging. He seemed as nervous as could be. And he spoke not a word of English. Knowing the neighbourhood as I did and now glad for the disturbance the police had made within the International Workmen's Club which abutted our *scène d'outrage*, we appealed to the membership for a translator.

Within moments our little party had grown by one, an obliging fellow performing the service gladly. "He first asks if he is in trouble, sirs."

"No, no trouble." I smiled. "Please reassure him of that."

Shifting his eyes around to the police and to his fellow countryman, our witness proceeded to speak.

"He says his name is Israel Schwartz. Of 22 Helen Street, Backchurch Lane. He says that a woman stood there, in the gateway to this yard and that a man had stopped to speak with the woman. It was then that the man tried to pull on the woman's arm, and she cried out, having fallen to the footway. Mr. Schwartz says he chose to cross the street rather than become involved in the altercation."

For this, Mr. Schwartz interrupted to point to where he had crossed to the other side. He added other gestures to his pantomime and continued to speak. Our translator said, "There he says he saw another man. Smoke— Smoking a pipe. Yes. He says the first man, the one who threw the woman to the ground then called out, 'Lipski.' The second then followed Mr. Schwartz. Scared, he hurried away, losing the man who followed him by the time he had reached the railway arch.

"He says that, when the cry for murder reached his ears, he chose to come back, believing he might have seen something that the police would find useful. He says he was first in Berner Street at a quarter of the hour."

"And the man he saw? The one accosting the woman?" I pressed.

Mr. Schwartz shrank from my intensity, and our helpful translator held hushed conference with him. "He says that the man was, perhaps, 30 years of age. One, two inches taller than the woman. He had on an overcoat and black felt hat—old. Old and with a wide brim. His hair was dark, and he had a small, brown moustache."

"Was he carrying anything? Had he a package?" Lestrade demonstrated with his hands.

"No. Nothing."

Mr. Schwartz shook his head and then mimed carrying something as though by a handle. "Orvos."

Our man from the Club obliged, "He says he had some sort of a black bag. The sort that a physician carries on his rounds."

"Well, however do you account for that, Holmes?" Lestrade turned to me.

"Neither man seen by our witnesses much resembles the other. Clearly our victim was a very sociable sort before she met her end. And considering her objectives—recall the contents of her hand, detective —she would have had cause to talk with many a man in this dim corner of London. I've no doubt that Mr. Schwartz and PC Smith are describing two different—"

"Detective!"

We both turned. Flushed and out of breath, a uniformed man rushed at us. With his arm outstretched he pointed wildly behind him to the gate of the yard. "Come quick. There's been another. Another Ripper murder and they want you to come at once. I've a four-wheeler waiting, sir."

Nearly collapsing under the strain of his message, the officer doubled over. Neither Lestrade or myself saw to the man's needs. We were off like a shot, intent on the scene of this the second slaying in one night.

TWO

CHAPTER 7

We rode westward along Commercial. Tense silence gripped my companions. As for myself, the noisome company of my reeling brain drowned out all other sound. I hardly saw High Street save as a reminder that the murderer might have passed that way—possibly while Lestrade and myself were running towards the scene of the first crime. The thought further sharpened my convictions to see this case through, whatever the cost.

Commercial gave way to Aldsgate, and at the intersection of Duke, our way grew too congested as to be passable. Lestrade and I alighted and ran towards the next block of Mitre Street. A nearby clock was striking a quarter past two when we met the City Police PC at the entrance to the square.

"What, are we holding an assembly here?" My barking command gained the attention of several other officers and detectives who had come to mill about the space. I gestured to the ground they were trampling. At their backs, a man rose to his feet. He wove through the throng, thrusting a hand in my direction. He said, "Ah, Inspector."

"Mr. Holmes, Doctor." I shook his hand. "This is Inspector Lestrade of Scotland Yard. And I am but a humble consultant brought in to offer fresh eyes upon the case. We were, as you can see from our state of dress, playing our part in watching the neighbourhood tonight."

The kindly face grew wan. "Doctor Sequeira. Called in from over on Jewry Street. She's over here. Brace yourselves, gentlemen."

We approached. The victim lay on her back, her arms at her sides. Her skirts had been hitched up around her waist, and the front of her dress was torn. She had been disembowelled, with her intestines thrown up across her right shoulder. Her throat was slashed much like her unfortunate predecessors. She had likely bled out within minutes. The blood had pooled beneath the body, and there was not much to see on that account. But it was her face which arrested each of our attentions. Mutilated beyond all reason, the victim's face had been horridly scored. Eyelids and nose. The cheeks. The lips and even the jaw—all bore their separate cuts.

"The brute."

"Indeed." I knelt, asking, "May I?"

Receiving the appropriate nod, I reached forward and gently turned the woman's face towards the light. The wound in her neck gaped.

Sequeira spoke up. "Cause of death would be haemorrhage from the throat. Death coming swiftly. The other wounds came after. I arrived within minutes of discovery and rigour mortis had not yet begun."

"Thank you, Doctor." I rose to my feet. "Two.

He had time for two and yet still escaped us. With all these men about."

"So there were two murders," Dr. Sequeira muttered. He noted my sharp glance, adding quickly, "Rumour's been rife this night."

I grunted and moved to inspect the larger space of the square itself. As I had already established through my pointed comment to the police presence, the ground had been made a muddy mess of foot traffic. But the entrances themselves might reveal something.

My efforts yielded little. Mitre Square possessed three points of entry. The largest I and Lestrade had passed through on our way in. If terrible Jack had been so bold as to leave that way, he was likely being questioned at this very moment. The back way was narrow and led out onto Duke Street. There I found evidence of the beat officer's measured steps as well as tracks from an unhurried couple—the smaller set clearly belonging to a woman. I made a mental note to inspect the victim's shoes and moved on. At the side entrance I had my luck. The man who had entered with the woman had left from that lane. Alone. Picking my way along, I followed the trail feeling hopeful for, perhaps, the first time since the case had been dropped at my door.

The narrow passage opened out on another square. At its centre, a manned fire station provided deterrent to hooliganism. Two gas lamps lit the space. Not a lot of opportunity to slink in and out unnoticed. Still, he had to have come this way, I argued with myself. But the two lanes leading to either side street yielded nothing. Either the man had come to his senses about covering his tracks or he had somehow found another way out.

Or I was plainly wrong.

Swearing under my breath, I returned to the narrow, covered alleyway and re-examined the footprints. A part of me wondered if I was falling to the grave error of twisting evidence to suit facts rather than thinking the proper way around. Desperation will do that.

The stride indicated a man of middle height—perhaps somewhere in the vicinity of five foot six or seven—the marks, a person of decent health, strength, and wealth. They were good shoes that had left the prints. I peered closer with my glass debating whether the signs of wear on the inner left sole indicated an injury or a long-held limp. In any event, it upped our chances a fair bit should we lay hands upon the killer in our sweep for suspects. I turned 'round to re-enter the square.

Lestrade waited for me there. He had with him a man wearing sergeant's stripes.

"Mr. Holmes, this is Sergeant Jones."

"How do you do." The sergeant's handshake was brisk and business-like. "I helped Inspector Collard make his check of the ground. I can confirm that neither he nor I found any signs of a struggle. And I have for you here the victim's effects."

I raised my eyebrows to the motley collection held out to me. He hurried to explain, "I only picked it up once the doctor gave me permission. We did not expect anyone else to look at the scene at that time, having already done our work."

"And we would have here . . . ?"

"Some buttons. A thimble. A tin containing two pawn tickets. Nothing particularly telling."

Quick strides took me back to where the body

still lay. I called out, "Was it arranged in any particular way?"

The pair hurried to follow. "None that I could tell, sir."

"Hmph. Thank you, sergeant." Frowning, I contemplated the mutilated corpse, seeing and dismissing in turns the various possibilities which sprang up under my observation. "A moment!"

The policeman turned back.

"Was her apron found like this?"

He looked. "Apron, sir? There's no apron there."

"Exactly."

"And yet, there are the strings that would suggest she had been wearing one." Lestrade sidled close.

Smiling, I looked to the Yard detective. "Lestrade, you've found an important clue. Or rather, shown us that one has gone missing."

A scuffle at the Mitre Street entrance broke our attention away from the scene at our feet. There a man in a bowler hat and long black coat, moustached and carrying a surgical bag, struggled between two policemen.

"Holmes!"

I ran towards the altercation. My mind raced. Watson? How the devil was he here?

"Watson!"

"Let the gentleman go. He's with us," Lestrade caught us up and issued his barked command.

The two officers released our friend. One of them explained, "Apologies, detective. But he matched our man in every point. Right down to the black bag. Had we known he was with—"

"Had you listened to me," Watson bristled, "you would have known."

"Ah, but a protestation of innocence is exactly

what our killer would have done in your circumstances, Doctor. The men are merely being thorough. And after the events of this night, I thank them for their vigilance, misplaced as it was in your case."

Watson's gape-mouthed disbelief followed me back into the square. I could feel his eyes on my back, his unasked questions damming up for later release. Well then, I had some of my own that I should like to put to him. But first we had a post mortem to attend. And as Doctor Watson had so willingly thrust himself into the scene, I would take the opportunity to observe and think before I accused as freely as had the PCs in Mitre Street.

For, while the sudden presence of the doctor was potentially explained away by his knowledge that I would be at the scene of this most recent tragedy, the rest of his appearance begged much explanation. I saw before me more than a man who merely matched the physical description of our Jack.

"And how is your patient, Watson?"

Did I sense a slight hesitation before his response? Did I see some small paling of his cheeks?

"My patient is quite fine, Holmes. But I have had a very long night." Were his words guarded?

I wondered. I wondered at it, same as I did the state of his clothes. While he had, of course, claimed a long night beside a sickbed, Watson's clothes were rumpled beyond forgiveness. And he had not merely neglected to change his shirt collar before coming out. No, he had done away with the old entirely, not bothering to replace it with a fresh. But what most concerned me, what chilled my heart and made me infinitely glad that we had interrupted the police before they had been allowed to arrest my friend . . . a dark splash of blood on the doctor's right shirt sleeve. A damning mark which I could espy peeping out from underneath the cuff of his overcoat. And I saw it. Because I had known to look for it.

DEVELOPMENTS

CHAPTER 8

After piling all together into a growler, we rode to the City Mortuary. A pre-dawn London passed by. Within a few hours it would be light, and the rest of the metropolis would wake to word of the new horrors in the East End while we non-victorious were reduced to poring over the macabre leavings of a madman.

"Is it true then, what they're saying? Two murders, Holmes?" Watson broke the silence.

I made no response save for a curt nod.

"Thank you for allowing me to come along to the post mortem. I am very sorry that I could not be with you last night."

My second acknowledgment was less than the first.

"I just happened to be passing through after seeing to my patient. Knowing your plans to be in Whitechapel, I found myself drawn to the place only to find the streets ringing with the cry of murder."

"And so came calling to offer your ever-capable assistance." I thawed at last. Beaming, he accepted the olive branch and contentedly sat back in his seat. Guilt blossomed in my chest. To think that I could so foolishly consider the worst from my friend.

Surely I had no call to bow out of this case. Not with the stakes at hand. But it was poison in my veins. Invisible carnage, the victim of which was my own reason.

Still, sitting at Watson's side, I kept thinking how I would very much have liked to get a look at that bag of his.

Golden Lane Mortuary received our little entourage with an eagerness that belied the circumstances. To the inimitable Doctor Watson, the small staff had great deference. And as for myself? One would have thought I had already caught and sentenced the East End villain for all the excitement my presence generated. Clearly they had read of our exploits at the end of last year.

All gaiety halted, however, when the body was brought in for its autopsy. Before leaving Mitre Square, we had received permission from the other doctor on the scene, a Doctor Gordon Brown, to perform our own preliminary examination. He, like Watson, had other commitments that required his attention elsewhere. The doctor would be coming to the mortuary to perform the official post mortem exam later in the day.

At the uncovering of the unfortunate woman's body, we were acutely reminded of the monster against whom we railed. Under the greater light of the mortuary the injuries seemed to grow more garish. Only Watson remained largely unmoved. I recalled that he had seen war firsthand. Still his jaw clenched, and his eyes gained a hard glint as he approached the mutilated corpse.

"How much of this comes from the transportation of the body?" he asked.

"Next to none," I replied.

At this, his shock gained a voice. The snapping sound of his sharp intake of breath echoed in the room.

"The bowels? They were drawn up like that?" Watson indicated the horrid arrangement of viscera and looked to me.

I nodded and moved to stand behind my friend. I did not quite like the shade his face had turned. "Lestrade?"

The inspector approached. "The victim at 29 Hanbury was in much the same condition. Disembowelled. Intestines drawn up over her shoulder. I have to ask, Doctor, has this woman's uterus been removed?"

"Why, I—!" Watson stared open-mouthed at the detective. He turned back to the body. "Honestly, it is a bit difficult to confirm that, considering the state the body is in. But . . . yes. It appears to have been cut out." He shuddered and turned away. "This is ghastly work, Holmes. I would stake my honour on a claim that the woman was dead from the gash across her throat but . . ."

"Doctor Brown will be along soon to do as he promised. I don't see the need for us to look further. Doctor Sequeira already formed his opinion at Mitre Square. Death came via a wound in the throat and was quick. She would not have had opportunity to cry out or struggle. This I can confirm from having examined the scene itself."

Having looked away from the victim, Watson was almost himself once more. Almost.

"Come, Watson. There's little more I can do

until daylight. And, as you said, it has been a long night for each of us."

Lestrade bade us farewell. He would send word of any further developments to Baker Street.

Though the sojourn to the Golden Lane Mortuary had taken us almost halfway home, the ride across town seemed to stretch on forever. Neither Watson nor myself proved to be in a talkative mood. Arriving at 221 at last, we deftly sidestepped Mrs. Hudson and made our way up into my apartment. There I rebuilt the fire while Watson moodily stared at the proceedings, finally giving a wistful smile and asking, "I could ring for coffee, maybe?"

"My preference would be rest. A fresh shirt might be in order as well. You'll find your things untouched." While I had expected my sardonic comment to produce some sort of reaction from my friend, I found myself unprepared for what actually occurred. Something flitted through Watson's face. Some terrible, unchecked emotion. It was an expression belonging to another man entirely: that secret self we all have but so rarely show to another. And then the furtive, guilty darkness was gone, an error swiftly corrected, a mask reassumed.

Without a word, Watson left the room, and it became my turn to stare into the fire while he hunted about for a change of clothing. Even after trading our partnership for a wife, the doctor still kept some belongings in my place. I made a mental note to look over them after he left.

"Oh, damn. I forgot my bag." Watson re-entered the sitting room with a look of bewildered annoyance upon his face. "Ah, well, no doubt Lestrade will keep it safe for me until I can get back to Golden Lane."

And thus was taken from me the other bit of investigation I had planned on while Watson slumbered. Considering the state of my raw nerves, I counted it a small blessing. With he on the couch and I on the chair by the hearth, we both found rest as the sky lightened on towards dawn.

Scarcely three hours had passed when a polite knock on the door set us both to waking.

"Sherlock? Urgent message for you from Mr. Lestrade. Ah, you're here too, Doctor." Mrs. Hudson entered to give over the telegram.

"Thank you, Mrs. Hudson. Oh, no breakfast. We won't have time." My eyes raked over the note. "Watson, get dressed."

"What is it?" he yawned.

"Lestrade. He says: 'Found apron. Message too. Come at once.' And then he gives an address."

" 'Message too'? Do you think there's been another letter?"

"I refuse to make any assumption until we've been to Goulston Street."

Together, Watson and I made from 221b. We hailed a hansom, and as we embarked, I saw a small figure dart into the space between the buildings across the way. Young Billy Wiggins with his report on Watson's activities of the past twelve hours. He would just have to wait until my return. With any luck, by that time my interest in Watson's private affairs would have sunk to mere curiosity on the part of a friend. Not that I had any such hopes at this point.

BLOODY APRON

CHAPTER 9

The day had dawned crisp and cool. Wispy clouds dashed through a bright autumnal sky. Mother Nature, it would seem, was in a forgiving mood. I predicted that Man would not be so lenient and prayed that Lestrade's discovery now meant we had the necessary evidence to further our case.

Riding side by side in the swaying cab, our blood singing under the urgency of our errand, I was reminded all the more of how I missed my previous partnership with Watson. Even without this case, a wedge had been driven between us by his moving away to James Street and finding a life all his own. Was I in the wrong then? I, who had not moved on and would have preferred nothing change?

I glanced sideways at my associate. He certainly looked eager enough. Eyes bright, head thrust forward, and a small smile playing about his lips pronounced him quite unfearful of what we might find at the end of Lestrade's thread. I sat back on the bench, lost to my thoughts as I reconsidered what thin facts we had in hand.

We reached Goulston Street as the first of the sun's rays brushed the building tops. Lestrade met us at the top of the lane. I alighted before the carriage had stopped moving, prompting a curse from the cabby. Watson followed a pace later, having mollified the driver with what I'm sure was a generous tip.

Lestrade appeared nervous. He spoke, "The missing apron was found by PC Long at about three. It was just lying there in the street, a bloodied lump of cloth. The cheek of it. He wanted us to come upon it."

"And the message?" I prompted.

"Well. Here's where we've a bit of trouble." I now realized that Lestrade's nerves were not merely uneasy. They quivered with anger.

"Mr. Holmes. What a pleasant surprise." Commissioner Warren blazed down the street towards us. "Had I known you would be coming to the scene of this latest puzzle, I wouldn't have sent the evidence onward to the Commercial Street Station."

Lestrade wanted to say something. He positively shook with it. Still he said nothing.

A moment later, I discovered why.

"What are those men doing?" I pointed and started off towards where I could see two policemen washing something off a brick wall.

"Mr. Holmes," Commissioner Warren called after me. "Mr. Holmes!"

The dark brickwork had been rendered darker still by the generous buckets of water which had been splashed over its surface. Brushes had done the rest.

"We wrote it down before we took it off," the commissioner huffed and paused to catch his breath. "I had a worry that it could incite a riot."

I stared, unbelieving, at the spot where our latest clue had only recently been thoroughly expunged.

"We can't even be certain it was him," Warren tried again.

I gave no sign I'd heard him. A waste. Such a terrible waste of opportunity.

"After that Lipski business——"

I turned on my heel and walked away.

"Holmes!"

"Watson, hail a cab. We're going to the Commercial Street Station."

"Holmes." Lestrade managed to match me stride for stride as I neared the end of the street. "When I sent you that wire I had no idea they would be so idiotic as to erase the evidence before you arrived."

"Cabbie!" I flung my arm out, and a hansom peeled off from the opposite kerb. It veered my way. "Watson?"

He hesitated. "Apologies, Lestrade." Watson's words were lost under my barked commands to our driver. We were off before more amends could be made.

Commercial Street slipped by as we progressed northward to the station.

"Really, Holmes, I do not think that display was entirely necessary."

I folded my arms and said nothing.

Used to my moods, Watson did the same.

We pulled up to the station. This time my steps were not so quick. I asked the driver to wait for us there for a half hour. If we did not return within that time, he could leave us to find our own ride back.

The Commercial Street Police Station was a narrow, three-storey building which ran the length of its triangular block. As such, it had the appearance of giving visitors a sidelong look, one that said "you'd better have business here," to those who approached. Watson and I were shown to an upstairs office where the latest clue in our case was being examined.

It was, as had been described to us by Inspector Lestrade, a blood-besmirched apron. Finally I had in my hand some sort of proof that our man Jack did not simply melt into thin air with the dawning of the day. Not that I indulged in such base fantasies. But here was an item that had travelled from Mitre Square, up through St. James'—where I had lost the scent—only to end up not half a dozen blocks northeast.

I needed to go back. But first, "Is the man available who found this?" I asked.

"He returned to the scene, sir."

I nodded and turned the bit of cloth over in my hand before spreading it out on the nearby table. "See, Watson, here where the strings were attached. If I recall correctly, this would match the piece of apron that our victim was missing. And the marks of blood smeared over it thus . . . If you grasped the bulk of it like so and drew a knife across, perhaps to clean your weapon—" I mimed the action as I spoke. "It does give us a better impression of what sort of implement the man uses for his killings. Mark well that stain, gentlemen. I thank you for your time. Come, Watson."

It occurred to me only as we left that my partner had said not one word while we were in the station. More taciturn than me, he allowed himself to be led back to the cab where I paused before giving our driver our destination. I turned to Watson then. "You desire to go home."

He opened his mouth to respond. Then shut it. This strange, skittish replacement for my steadfast and feeling friend remained unreadable for one long moment. Foolishly, I pressed. "Your patient—"

"Home. Yes. Mary will be wondering." Watson moved to disembark, then turned back. Indecision rippled across his features. More words were left unsaid between us, and he gave me a thin smile. "Goodbye, Holmes."

That same indecision seemed to plague his steps as he walked away to hail a cab that would take him back to Paddington. Intently, I watched the slump of his tired shoulders, the slight meandering path his feet struck as he crossed the road, and weighed what I saw. I almost followed him. As a friend and for no other reason. Instead I engaged in a bit of behaviour that, I'll admit, seemed almost foolish at the time and gave my heart no small amount of pain.

Beckoning a boy who lounged on the corner, I flashed a bright coin. The youth loafed forward with alacrity, and I was pleased to discover that I did, indeed, know the lad, if distantly. One of Wiggins' lieutenants. A sometime member of my own Baker Street division of police who could see and remain unseen, hear and retain the anonymity and inno-cence of any boy on the street.

"Yes, sir?"

"That man?" I pointed. "I'd like you to follow him. To the ends of the earth if need be. But follow him and send word to Baker Street as soon as he settles."

"Yes, Mr. Holmes." The shilling disappeared,

and the lad dashed off. I set my conscience aside, rapped my signal to the driver perched above, and settled back into my bench for the return to Goulston Street.

I had not been gone long enough for Lestrade to have left the scene of the apron's finding. If he found it odd that I returned Watson-less, he did not comment. Nor did he have time, for I threw myself into my work without pause upon arrival at the newly washed section of brickwork which had only recently held our latest clue.

"I have waiting for you the man who discovered both apron and writing." Lestrade strove to keep pace as I darted about the place. Footprints at this late hour would be of next to no use. And already the Ripper had proven himself more than capable of anticipating that line of investigation on my part. I needed to establish angles and lines of sight—areas of illumination and shadow present during the overnight. Establish for myself what the man would have seen as he fled the scene of his outrage and thereby, hopefully, project myself into his thoughts. Had he come upon Goulston Street at random? Had he fled the vicinity only to double back so that he might enjoy the frantic efforts of those bent on his capture? Was our Jack the Ripper from somewhere nearby, and if so, in what direction did he reside? My mental map was expanding by the minute. Details filled in with surprising speed. But to what end? Lestrade and myself had, only last night, established how honeycombed this district was. If the Ripper—when, I corrected—strikes again, is there any discernible pattern I might use to prevent another tragedy?

My measured steps brought me to a uniformed

PC. To his credit he waited for my attentions patiently, even managing to assume something of bored tolerance on his tired features without crossing over into frank rudeness.

"Police Constable Long?" I gave him my consideration at last.

"Mr. Holmes? Mr. Lestrade here says I should tell you all that I know."

"That would be most welcome, yes." I smiled warmly, noting for myself various points of his outfit and posture as I did so.

"I came down Goulston at a few minutes to three, and that's when I saw the bit of cloth lyin' in the road. I could see straight off that it was dipped in blood or something like blood. Picking it up, I just knew it was a part of a woman's apron. And that's when I saw the writing on the wall right near."

"Had you passed this spot on your previous circuits?"

"Yes. And I'll swear that it wasn't there until three when I happened by again."

"And do you know when your previous walk down Goulston was?"

"It would have been at about twenty past two. Street was clear then."

"And the message chalked upon the wall?"

"I only saw it once I saw the apron, sir. I think I would have noticed it, even in the dark. It had to be him. It had to be from the murderer."

I smiled past the man's presumption. "And the message itself? What did it say?"

"I wrote it down, sir. Here— 'The Juwes are the men that will not be blamed for nothing.' I blew my whistle and set about searching the sidewalk and all the staircases that led from that entrance."

"And found nothing."

"Nothing. Not a drop of blood. Nothing to suggest that our man was being anything other than extraordinarily careful."

"Suggesting, therefore, that both apron and message were deliberately left for us to discover. And after this finding of nothing further, you left a man in charge and brought the apron to the station only to then dutifully return here to the scene."

The PC nodded and suppressed a yawn.

"I can see you've been delayed long enough so as to give me your witness personally. If I may? I would like to first copy down the message for my own use, as I can see there is an interesting spelling of 'Juwes' in the message. That is how it appeared to you? Exactly thus?"

Here the man drew himself back to something akin to alertness. "Yes, sir. My spelling's not all bad as that. Though from what I hear tell, our Ripper isn't too sharp on his letters."

"Yes, that must be it," I mused, understanding now why Commissioner Warren had been so desirous of having the inflammatory message removed when he had. "Thank you for your statement of facts, constable."

When he departed, another rose to take his place. Lestrade, still present in spite of his own lengthy stretch, introduced us. Detective Constable Halse, he had been both at the scene over in Mitre Square and left in charge of the graffiti in Goulston after the apron's discovery. He began his own statement without preamble, "He's wrong, you know."

"Who? The commissioner?" Lestrade fairly bristled. I raised my eyebrows.

"No. PC Long. I stood by that message up until

88

they decided to wash it off. I even suggested they take off the top bit and leave the rest until we could photograph it." He puffed his chest in pride.

"And the note actually read as . . . ?"

" 'The Juwes are not the men that will be blamed for nothing.' Long moved the 'not,' you see."

"Ah." Lestrade turned inquisitive eyes my way. I was busy copying the second message below the first.

"Thank you, Long. That will be all."

I spent the remainder of the morning and afternoon going over the blocks surrounding Mitre Square and Goulston Street, keeping also within my mental map Dutfield's Yard off Berner Street where our double horror had begun the night before.

The boldness. The arrogance! It rankled me to think that, with every policeman in the area looking for the Ripper, while Inspector Lestrade and I were lost in poring over every inch of Mitre Square, Jack had taken upon himself a third errand. He had been ahead of us every step of the way and afterward had lingered to gloat. The bloody apron was proof enough of that.

Then for Watson to show up in the midst of everything. Watson with his own strange secret.

I recalled that I had answers to at least one of these twin mysteries waiting for me at home and so returned there.

THE BAKER STREET IRREGULARS

CHAPTER 10

An urchin stood in the front hall of 221B Baker Street. Self-conscious and shuffling his feet, he had withstood several appeals from the landlady to simply leave his word there for Mr. Sherlock Holmes and be off. It was my own informant, the lad I had set upon Watson's retreating form earlier in the morning.

"Ah, young Perth." I recalled his name at last as I beckoned him forth. In my hand I had for him the second coin which I had withheld until services rendered.

He pocketed the payment and then paused. Had I not known the character and needs of his ilk, I would have half suspected he wanted to give back his fee. Thrusting his hands behind him, he scowled. "I lost 'im. Roundabouts Baker's Row. 'M sorry, Mr. Holmes."

An unexpected development. I blinked. "Baker's Row?"

He gave a furious nod.

"Ran into a bit of trouble and had to dodge a

PC's attention. When I looked up, his cab was gone amongst the rest." He repeated his apologies and hung his head.

"You've done well, Perth." I pasted a smile to my face, lest he further misinterpret my displeasure. "I hadn't considered the size of my request, having anticipated that Dr. Watson would be going to where he had said he would."

It was a test. The boy passed.

"Oh no, sir. He did go off in the other direction. At first. I managed to follow him all the way to Golden Lane where he stopped off. His cab waited for him, and I followed again. He went on for several blocks westward before abruptly turning north. A block later he had swung back around onto his initial route, but he was now going east."

At this I frowned. Such subterfuge.

And for what, Watson?

"And are you certain you followed the right man?"

"Yes, sir. Absolutely certain."

"Curious," I mused. Remembering that I had a guest, I refocussed my eyes. "Thank you very much, Perth. That will be all."

He backed towards the door, hesitant. It drew my attention once more, and I asked my question through raised eyebrows.

The boy paused and then blurted, "Don't tell Billy."

This concerned me. My frown deepened.

Perth shuffled his feet. "He'll be disappointed."

My brief fears were allayed, and I saw where I stood in the hierarchy of things. Disappoint Chief Wiggins? Oh, we'd best not!

I dismissed the boy, mollified Mrs. Hudson, and

had just made it back to my apartments when the bell rang in the hallway below.

"Like the troubled sea, for it cannot rest," I sighed and went to answer the summons.

"You ought to find yourself a bit of sleep, Mr. Holmes."

"I should say the same to you, Lestrade." I ushered the inspector in.

He sat heavily upon my couch without invite. He looked utterly used, and for a moment I wondered if he intended to take my advice on the matter of rest right then and there. I sat opposite and waited.

At length he swivelled his gaze to meet mine and said, " 'The Juwes are the men that will not be blamed for nothing.' "

"Or, 'The Juwes are not the men that will be blamed for nothing,' " I quoted the alternate back at him.

"It makes no sense either way," the inspector grumbled. He sat forward in his seat. "You don't think . . . No, even I'll admit that's a bit of a reach."

"You must speak your theories aloud if you'd like me to test them. My powers don't quite reach to the levels of mind reading," I commented drily.

He snorted. "Yet, Mr. Holmes. Yet. I would not be surprised if next week you could line up five men ready for the gallows and tell me each of their separate thoughts in flowing monologue."

"The thoughts of the condemned are rarely original. Such would not be altogether too difficult," I quipped. "But, to return to the present. You're stuck on either the mystery of the creatively-spelt 'Juwes' or our wandering 'not.' "

"The latter is likely a clerical error. The sentence is fairly ridiculous wherever you put that word. But the former . . ." Lestrade wagged a finger. "I was wondering if our Jack creature is, in fact, a Frenchman. There are distinct possibilities in *juives*."

I flinched and sidestepped the desire to remind Lestrade of the perils in assigning the nationality of a man based on the mere presence of a scrawled word upon a wall. Instead, I took the high road and countered, "Or one might consider the Masonic significance of the spelling. J-U-W-E-S. And as at least two of the women slain had their vitals lifted up and placed across their shoulder after the manner of a ritual slaughter, it does bear consideration."

"Does it?" Lestrade's eyes had widened considerably.

I waved my hand. "That's merely one of any number of options which an educated man possessed of a suspicious turn of mind may invent."

"Oh."

We sat in sullen silence for several minutes. We each had our complaints. We were both exhausted beyond measure. At any moment one or the other of us might get upon his companion's last nerve.

"So there really is nothing to be learnt from this latest other than to confirm that, once again, this Jack the Ripper character is pointedly thumbing his nose at the police."

"And enticing the press, yes. Had the graffiti remained, I might have ascertained the man's height, where and how he stood as he chalked the message, and, perhaps, facts about the hand which had writ the message."

"Points we've already gleaned from his letter and from various eyewitnesses," Lestrade countered. "This case, Holmes. It goes 'round and 'round."

"We will have him, Lestrade. We will," I promised. Fool that I am.

As though sensing the helplessness of our position and the frustrations that it sparked, Lestrade rose to leave. I saw how terribly spent he looked and knew he stood as a mirror to my own exhaustion.

"Thank you, Mr. Holmes," he managed and then was gone.

A half an hour later I had burnt through half a toe of my strongest tobacco and had resorted to my Stradivarius. But even in my aimless scraping I found little solace. The problem of Jack the Ripper was eating at me, burning at my soul like acid in a tray. I moved to the window and looked out upon an equally sullen London. Oddly, my mind chose to travel not upon the worn paths of my current case, but, instead, decided to relive others of my past. So many criminal elements identified and thwarted. Dozens of inconceivable designs of pure malice unravelled. Each a sign that justice would prevail. But Jack the Ripper? It was as though he had read them all and found not deterrent but instruction. A pupil to my own school of crime, he chose to play bits back at me, a rote recitation of pure evil.

Along such lines of thought lay destruction. I passed my desk and, checking the time, pocketed my watch on the way to yet another long bout with my pipe. I glanced out the window again, thinking that perhaps it was high time I eat something today when the sight of a scuffle below my doorway caught my eye. Of the two young ruffians, I recognised one.

Running downstairs, I moved to separate the boys. Billy Wiggins. And a lad I did not know.

"This'n 'ere's been followin' me!" Billy complained, scowling at the unknown youth.

The second boy tried to make a break for it, but I held fast to his collar. I craned my neck. No constable in sight and the street had but the fitful traffic of a Sunday evening. The interrogation might yet go unnoticed, and we would have our answers. "Followed. How far?"

Billy gulped, ashamed. "Not sure. At least as far as Bishop's Road Bridge."

A place not far from Watson's house. This was bad.

"Who are you working for?" How I managed to keep my voice level, I may never know.

"I'm just out walking."

"Who?" This demand, I will admit, was less steady than the first.

"Nobody. That boy's a liar."

"Billy," I addressed my intermediary. Perhaps it was a mere misunderstanding. I hoped.

But my man was earnest, explaining, "I stopped twice. Went into a shop, an alleyway, and even doubled back, sir."

"Who? Who asked you to follow him?" This time my question came with a none-too-gentle shake.

He gulped. This time his protestation came quiet, scared, "I cannot say."

"Cannot or will not?"

"I cannot say, sir. Please."

Billy leapt on my captive, ready to mete the punishment I had stayed. My other hand collared my young informant, and I was left in the rather perilous position of gaoler when a policeman hurried our way.

" 'Ere now, what's this then?"

"He's a dirty rotten thief and I tol' 'im so," Billy

abruptly changed tack, sniffling and wiping his nose. The other boy glared.

"See here—" the constable began his scolding.

"Goods are in 'is pocket. Look." Billy's picture of innocence won his freedom from my hand. "I tried to warn the bloke back on the corner and this'n ran. This gentleman helped me stop him."

The constable relieved me of my charge and ordered him to turn out his pockets. True to Billy's claim, the boy revealed himself to be in possession of a handsome gold watch. He seemed as surprised as the policeman and immediately set about blubbering his excuses. " 'Nough of that. I'll get the truth from you back at the station. You, boy, run on now. And you, sir, my apologies for the disturbance."

"Not at all, constable." I smiled, innocent as Billy. "I am, in fact, more than willing to try to find the owner of that watch. It is otherwise a rather hopeless case, would you not agree?"

"Why, you're—! You're not—!" For the first time, the man seemed to realize where he stood and with whose aid he had managed to catch the thief of the century. His eyes bulged as he looked to me, then up at the building behind us, and back at me. "You're Mr. Sherlock Holmes! From *Beeton's*!"

Watson's folly. My smile thinned but did not disappear entirely. "Yes. And you can be sure that if I cannot locate the owner of that watch, I will contact you."

"Not a problem at all, sir." Grinning, the policeman handed over the heavy gold watch. "The wife'll never believe me. Mr. Sherlock Holmes." Shaking his head admiringly, he sauntered away with his felon in tow.

I turned to the narrow alleyway where Billy had

slipped unseen. "Am I to take it that Watson never came home?"

"No, sir. Should I go back?"

I debated. "Send someone else in your stead. I'm curious if it was you the boy was meant to follow or merely anyone in my employ."

Nodding, he moved to run off into the evening gloom.

"Oh, and Billy?" At my question, Wiggins hunched in alarm. "How did that watch end up in that boy's pocket?"

He turned back to beam his stagy innocent smile. "I cannot say."

Placing his hands behind his head he whistled off down the street.

I chuckled to myself at the cheek of it. It was only after I went upstairs, found my dressing gown and slippers, and sat myself before the fire that I took up the stolen watch only to find that the blessed thing was my own timepiece. Thoroughly undone at last, I threw my head back and laughed heartily and long. Scotland Yard's finest could learn a thing or two from young Billy Wiggins.

THE NAME SHERLOCK HOLMES

CHAPTER 11

I awoke on October 1st, 1888, to clear skies and an equally clear head. I had my plan formulated. The machine of my mental faculties had been re-oiled and set aright. At present, two cases occupied me. Firstly, I should go calling upon Scotland Yard to hear what I might of the latest in the Ripper killings. Secondly, I was to pursue the track begun when I set my irregulars upon Watson's movements.

My friend had a secret. I yet refused to think it a dark one.

The morning papers soon conspired to wreck my simple ambitions for the day. Setting down to breakfast, I quickly scanned the whole of the reports on the East End business, of which there were many. None contained reference to either Watson or myself. We had been kept out of the affair as requested. The *Daily News*, however, contained a blunder that had me throwing down my napkin in a fit of pique. They had, in their infinite stupidity and quest to sell more papers than their rivals, printed the whole of the Ripper's missive to the Central News.

"Don't they see that's what he wanted them to do?" I cried, seizing the offending sheet and shaking it. The futility of my actions dawned on me then. Rising, I abandoned my breakfast. Minutes later I was traveling southward to Scotland Yard. The peevish part of my brain smirked to think of the aggravating events of yesterday morning with regards to the evidence in Goulston Street and my own reaction to such. I had half a mind to shake Commissioner Warren's hand next I saw him, if only to reward his accidental genius at having robbed the press of their next sensational printing of Jack's reported communiqué. It would not do to bow to the Ripper's ever-insistent search for fame.

The offices of the Metropolitan Police were buzzing like a hive when I arrived at Whitehall. Just as the mention of my name opened many doors, I was escorted into the centre of the action by mentioning Lestrade's. He had been expecting me, apparently.

"Good morning, Mr. Holmes. I had hopes I might see you before the morning's inquest on Elizabeth Stride—she's the Berner Street victim." Lestrade beckoned me forward. "I trust you saw the morning's papers?"

I assented that I had.

"Kept you out of it as we had agreed. But here's a new puzzle for you." He reached forward and gingerly picked up from the desk a postcard. My brow furrowed as I took in the address on the front. "The Central News Office, London City E.C. Postmark of October 1." I turned it over and read:

. . .

I was not codding dear old Boss when I gave you the tip, you'll hear about Saucy Jacky's work tomorrow double event this time number one squealed a bit couldn't finish straight off. Had not time to get ears off for police thanks for keeping last letter back till I got to work again.

Jack the Ripper

I frowned and turned the card back over. "Posted today?"

"Doesn't take a mind like yours to know something's wrong with that note. Man at the post office thought it'd do more good in our hands than that of the press and so passed it on to us rather than directing it as addressed. That Jacky claims a double event is old news now, of course. But someone would have had to have been very fast to work up a hoax in answer to that first letter, word of it having only hit the papers just this morning."

"Oh, I agree that this does not carry in it the scent of fakery." Squinting, I held the postcard up to the light. "I do believe it the work of the same man. And I believe that he is, again, working to hide his identity through grammar and a careful alteration of his handwriting. It's as though . . ."

"Yes, Mr. Holmes?"

I shook my head and handed over the postcard. How could I not be forthcoming with my thoughts on this? I compromised, "It's as though this murderer has studied how the police work. Just as he has shown us his awareness of how the press operates. He is not a fool, nor is he doing these killings carelessly. He takes risks, to be certain. I would bet that a fair amount of his illicit thrill comes from that danger to his liberty and life."

"As with the other, he probably wrote and then held on to his letter for a day or so. Wanted to see if word would reach the papers before sending it off." Lestrade's face grew troubled. "Well, how are we to do something about this with him anticipating our moves so neatly?"

I made no immediate reply. The morning's post-card offered no direct threat. And if the established pattern held, it would be days—perhaps weeks—before Jack struck again. If so, we had opportunity to turn this game against he who orchestrated it. But that was only if he hadn't already anticipated such and planned accordingly.

If, if, if . . .

"Been thinking of setting up men to mark who buys the papers. If this Jack character wants to gloat over his notoriety, he's likely buying up every issue and scouring the headlines on Whitechapel."

I snorted my derision. "If buying the daily news and following the activities of the criminal element is now cause for suspicion, you may as well clap me in irons, Inspector."

"Or your Dr. Watson," he laughed.

At a sharp look from me, Lestrade corrected himself. "Yes, I know it's foolish. But it tells you where we're at in this whole thing. Our wits' end, Mr. Holmes. And no doubt this Jack knows it."

I considered. "Have you the first note at hand? I should like to compare the two."

"Certainly."

I waited as the first of Jack the Ripper's letters was produced. Through a side by side comparison, I was fairly certain that the writer of both that first letter and this most recent postcard were the same. Sitting down, I frowned over the grisly pair. At length, Lestrade harrumphed. "I'm sorry, Holmes. But with the inquest coming, I really ought to be on my way."

At his gentle interruption, I surfaced from my thoughts. The police headquarters coalesced around me, and I blinked. I needed more time. And while I hadn't neglected to leave home without my glass, I required better lighting than this if I were to make use of it.

As though sensing my impatience, Lestrade offered, "You may take it with you for further consideration. Though I will have to send someone 'round later to collect it."

"I'm well aware that time is of the essence in this case." I gave a small smile and thanked him for his accommodation.

"Heavens know you've helped us a time or two." It might have been the nicest compliment Lestrade had paid me while in the presence of others. 'Twas a pity I found myself hiding from him my true feelings on the case. But then the police were, at his admission, grasping at straws. Far be it from me to misdirect their efforts over so thin a conjecture. Besides, I'd look a fool making the suggestion which lived at the back of my mind.

I returned home to find Watson waiting for me within our old apartments.

Faced with no real reason not to, I updated him on the case. Through it all his frown deepened, and his agitation grew. My heart swelled within me to watch the man fall, at last, to those deep feelings for which my old friend was so susceptible. I ended on a recitation of the morning's postcard at which John gave vent to his emotions by crying out, "What monster is this!"

" 'Tis a monster of our own making, Watson."

"I am to blame, Holmes."

The instinct to correct him rose up within me. Yet I said nothing. After all, his denial of the Croydon business still lay between us. That alongside the parade of small but conspicuous deceptions which had since followed.

I considered his presence here. If I could get him to talk freely and without careful consideration, then perhaps I might guide him into revealing what he had been about when he had not gone home after Goulston Street. Check and mate, as it were. But no, the fire that had stirred in John Watson burnt itself out, and a moody silence reigned in the sitting room of 221B.

Impatient, I reached for my pipe. Settling his gaze back upon me, Watson's face cleared, and he said, "Still. We might yet make it right. I thought that, perhaps, we might ride together to the inquest for Mrs. Stride and—"

"No, Watson. Neither of us shall be testifying in this case."

"You've asked that we not?"

"No," I answered drily. "It was Lestrade who made the request."

"And why not?" Watson started forward in his chair, incensed. "Surely our assistance carries some weight—yours if not my own."

Here was something of interest. I pushed. "They thought it best that neither of our names appear in connection with this little puzzle. After *A Study in Scarlet*—"

"Holmes!" Watson collapsed backward into his

chair, stricken. "Have I . . . I have not inadvertently ruined your consulting services?"

"Changed it, perhaps. Attached a degree of sensationalism where cold logic ought to have prevailed." I waved off his concerns, though the danger now lay within my own emotions. He had struck a nerve, after all. "People seem to think I am some sort of magician, a conjurer of clues. And there is, of course, the question of discretion."

Watson groaned. "I am sorry, Holmes."

I moved to reassure him. "If anything, it frees me for better cases. Those who understand crime now know what I can do within its trail. The Yard, for example, had no hesitation calling upon me for this series of murders."

"While the murderer himself uses pages from your cases to suit his ends. I cannot help but feel implicated by his threat to send the ears of his victims to the police." Here Watson set his gaze to the fireplace and became as unreadable to me as stone.

I tried a new tack. "I should have thought our limited involvement and credit welcome to your own easy domesticity. After all—"

"My wife, Holmes, is of all people a champion for the work we do here! She having benefited first-hand from the justice you brought to her own trou-bled situation. In fact, she—" Watson bit off his tirade and, having risen to his feet, looked to the clock in the room. "Goodness! I shall be late. Even if you do not think it worth our while to have our hand known in this case, I feel it my duty to be present at that poor woman's inquest today. No, Holmes. I do not need a chaperone. I will remain a silent spectator to the proceedings. My quest for fame does not reach as far as you believe. But I will say this: justice is being sorely tried. And I wish to God that I had never—"

He shook his head and said no more save to leave me with a quiet, "I'm sorry, Holmes."

I wanted to be glad for his leaving and leaving in such a way and with such a clearly established direction for his steps that I might call upon Mrs. Watson without fear of interruption. For I had yet to follow up on the unaccounted-for movements reported to me by Wiggins and Perth.

But in his wake I only felt despondency. Distracting, annoying, frustrating emotional turmoil over my friend's words and actions. I turned my eye to where Jack's letter lay upon my desk. Work. Work hardened me. Exertion would crystallize my thoughts and make me useful once more. I moved. I reflected.

What was it about this letter that struck my mind so? It was not the sensational fact that it existed. No. In my decade as a consulting detective, I had been exposed to far more unusual facets of crime than this. Watson had chronicled many of them, though the public at large knew of just the one case. The one case we had argued over mere minutes ago.

Confounded, I ceased my useless rummaging of the attic of my mind. I paused, I might have even stopped breathing as I waited for the notion to come at me. Holding the paper up to the desk lamp, I relaxed my mind. An exercise in will, I paradoxically had to let go before I could grasp at what whispered itself into my brain.

I turned the letter over and set the strong lamp to shining upon the back of the page. My magnifying glass aided my eyes in seeing the collection of tiny black marks which dotted the paper. They could have been specks of dirt but were not. Again I held the letter up to the light, confirming that the points were aligned as I thought.

The disparate collection of black dots and lines backed the crimson words of writing upon the front of the paper. Clearly the writer of said letter had written it while the paper lay upon a sheet of newsprint or magazine page. The pressure of the pen on top had led to a partial transference of the print below.

I frowned, thinking of Lestrade's words. Grasping at straws. So what if this Jack the Ripper had written atop another piece of paper? Unless that paper were something addressed to the killer himself, some incriminating piece of evidence to act as a convenient signpost, this clue had as little to tell me as all the rest.

And here was where my quiet concentration of mind paid its dues. Tilting the page left and right, I knew at once what had been bothering me these past several days. Some secret part of my brain had seen the damning detail from the first. And in its wake a disquiet; a sickness deep within my heart, my soul.

Stricken, I dashed to my window-side bookshelf and rifled through the collection therein. I unearthed a bent little magazine, published from around the time of last Christmas. *Beeton's*. *A Study in Scarlet*. I flipped through its thin pages, my fervour a combination of maddened frenzy and fearful hope. Oh, to be wrong . . . I would glory in it. I would crow.

There it was. Stangerson. Joseph Stangerson. Along with Enoch Drebber, Mr. Jefferson Hope . . . and my own name, Sherlock Holmes. It was that which had snagged at my mind. For a man can hardly help but recognise his own name, even writ piecemeal as this was.

I tilted the page; held it up to the light. And in placing Jack's letter in front of it, the little bits and bobs come together to make a whole.

Dumbfounded, I sat back in my chair and stared, unseeing, for I do not know how long. I had before me, discovered through the strangest coincidence of memory and fate, the very page that had lain under the Ripper's letter to the Central News Agency. Page 49 of *Beeton's Christmas Annual*. Words penned and published by Dr. John Watson last year, read with interest by the public, and then almost immediately discarded by all with the wrappings and trappings of the season. Watson had lamented that there were almost no copies left of his one moment of glory, at how quickly his star had set.

Well, Jack the Ripper had not forgotten. That or . . .

MARY

CHAPTER 12

I shuddered, unable—even then—to believe the worst of my friend. The net had not yet closed; the evidence, while suggestive, was hardly damning. Not that the police would adopt so tolerant a stance, desperate as they were. For everything spoke against my friend. Everything save for his character. Ten years at Baker Street; a decade of shared dangers and passions. He was—admit it, Holmes—as close to me as I would likely ever allow anyone.

Why I pursued the game, I well knew. But why had Watson? Why, upon day one, had he agreed so readily to be my flatmate? I, who he had hardly known and who most found nigh intolerable. How had he ingratiated himself into my life? What with myself being a person who tolerated the excitements and base normalcy of others with as much patience as was given me. And why would this medical man take so soundly to chronicling my work? Studying it, embracing it though he himself had little talent and interest in its finer points. He was no mere admirer, no. He had written down every word, enhancing and expanding upon the truth of it all as he went. Dr. John Watson was no spectator. In electing himself my mouthpiece, he had elevated himself.

And thus my two cases were related, intertwined so deeply that it was on me to unravel them lest Lestrade and his ilk fix upon the points that had so engaged my brain. This Jack the Ripper may inexplicably know my methods, might anticipate them and play my own game against me, but so too did the Yard. They had tutored under that self-same school.

I had but one move left at this juncture, and I glanced at the clock, thinking hard. To call unannounced at the Watson residence would simply have to be forgiven. Hopefully, Mary was in at this hour. For I had a limited time in which John was to be engaged elsewhere.

And if he was home instead of at the inquest for Mrs. Stride? Well, then I should have my answers directly.

I set off for James Street having fired off a quick telegram to the Yard with instructions that a man might be sent to collect the evidence Lestrade had loaned me. I no longer had need for it. The letter had burnt itself into the backs of my eyelids so that I saw the Ripper's words even when I closed my eyes.

Having considered myself insensitive to the horrors to which my profession subjected me on a regular basis, I distrusted this new weakness within my emotional makeup. I had no frailties! Food and drink. Love of comfort. Love . . . of any kind. All these stood as distractions when an intellectual problem was at hand. I had worked hard to eliminate all potential liabilities from myself. That same careful training, this commitment to my mind, had been the source of endless badgering from both Mrs. Hudson and Dr. Watson over the years.

And had, in turn, created gaping holes within my careful armour. Their regard, their trust, had eroded my resolve. This was, of course, not new information for me. I knew how dependent I had become upon Mrs. Hudson—domestically speaking, of course. And Watson's taking a wife the previous year had been a blow that had required many months for me to overcome. This along with more bottles of my "seven-per-cent" cocaine solution than I would care to admit.

Fear was new, however. Fear for my friend and of my friend. And for myself should I follow this trail to its end and find, at long last, that crime's tragedy touched my life in such a fashion.

I was wrong. I had to be. It would not be the first time—whatever Watson liked to say in his little chronicles of our cases together. It would not be the last.

And Mrs. Watson would prove it so within minutes. I would be made the happiest of fools this day. With a lighter heart, I sprang from the cab. Eyeing the house with its stone facade of even-faced calm, I knew—knew!—that John could not be at fault for these murders in the East End. It was absurd that I should have even given such a theory my time.

Ascending the steps, I rang and waited. A perfectly respectable servant let me into the perfectly respectable home. Giving over my hat and stick, I waited in the sitting room, eased by the quiet comforts my friend enjoyed. The Watson home was about as far from 221b Baker Street in flavouring as was the seaside from The Scrubs. A new guilt shivered through me. I ought to have come calling more often these past months. This was not the errand which should have brought me 'round at last. What sort of friend was I?

Mary's entrance pulled me from my bleak thoughts.

"Sherlock." She smiled and rushed forward to greet me. "Whatever is the matter?"

Ah, here was the partner truly worthy of my friend. Miss Morstan had been a near model client. I smiled, as much an attempt at putting her worries at ease as a re-disciplining of my emotions. My questions were simple. The answers likely just as. With John's practice, his hours and his callings away from home were oftentimes as varied and far-reaching as my own.

"And how are you, Mrs. Watson?"

The woman gave a mild shake of her head at my formality. "It's been a warm summer. John and I had wanted to get away to the country but never had the chance."

I steeled myself, unnecessarily, of course, and asked, "And how is his practice?"

"Not as busy as it had been in the spring. We've had such fine weather. Warm but fine. Healthful." She paused the conversation to wait through the bringing of tea. I waved off the hospitality and leaned forward in my chair, intense in spite of my efforts to the contrary. If Mary noted my shift in attention, she did not show it. "You, Sherlock, have been keeping my husband very busy."

"Me." Surprise rippled through me, a thrill which left me cold.

"At the outset of our marriage I had expected I

should have to share John with you and your work, of course. And as I said, with his medical practice having lagged of late, it gives him something to do. The excitement he gets from his going on your little adventures . . . ?" She shook her head. "So long as you continue to give him back to me unscathed at the end of each case, I'll tolerate the chronic absence of my husband to his old apartments at Baker Street."

I became obliquely glad for my having already given Mary my rapt attention. Watson? My absent friend had been going on cases with me? For how long had this been going? I tested the waters. "Has he said much about our latest case?"

"He saves all his recounting for his scribbles. But he's never been so cruel as to forget to tell me when he's staying at 221."

The terrible tremor within my soul repeated its cruel urging. My throat dried and my pulse quickened. Keenly on the scent of Watson's secret, I pushed. Too hard, I'll admit. But such are the pitfalls of profound regard. I said, "Watson has not stayed overnight at Baker Street since you were married last fall."

There was no mistaking now how things stood. I had ventured into the truth at last.

Mary gave a strangled sob and then crumpled.

I rushed to her side, cursing my stupidity. Had I but known how deep the lie had gone . . .

Emitting a small noise, she waved me off. "Oh, I knew it. I knew there was something wrong. But as his wife, I dared not voice my misgivings lest John think I did not trust him."

"Surely there's an explanation for it. A patient's need. Or, perhaps, it's mere misunderstanding."

"No, no misunderstanding," Mary cried and rose to her feet. She swayed and put a hand to her head. "What a fool I've been. What a silly fool."

"Mary." I grasped her elbow, lending her my strength. "Miss Morstan, you must tell me all."

"I'm not certain I have much to tell outside of a woman's instinct."

"Mary." My gaze steadied her, and I let go her arm. I remained ready, however, lest she fall into a swoon at last. "You may see it as a condemnation of your husband but, truly, your words now may prove his saving in the end. If you trust me——"

"I trust you, Mr. Sherlock Holmes. As should John. As I thought he had." She sank back into her chair, a poised and calm woman once more, though her eyes sparkled as she continued, "How could he lie to us both? And where—where has he been? If you're here and asking these questions of me, what is it he's been telling you?"

Mary met my gaze with a hardened resolve. She could take whatever news I had to give her. Though such romantic entanglements were never to be my path in life, I could see why John loved this woman. Miss Mary Morstan was a rare specimen. Watson's allying with her made me proud, indeed.

"Doctor Watson has been rather absent from my life these many long months," I began, my voice even and as devoid of judgment and emotion as was my wont. "As such, I cannot say upon which occasions he may or may not have been misleading you as to his whereabouts. But I, myself, have reason to believe that all is not well with John, and this is what has led me to your door, as you have so astutely observed."

White-lipped, she nodded. "I can recall no less

than six occasions within the past two months that he has claimed to be with you after having been absent from home for a minimum of twenty-four hours."

"Can you recall which days in particular?" I had my note-book out and ready.

"Not all the dates, I'm sorry. But I know for certain that he's been absent—with you, I thought—on the night of April 2nd, July 29th, August 6th, and, most recently, this past Saturday evening. Having read in the papers the next morning of what had happened that night, I did not think to question it. I knew Sherlock Holmes could not sit idly by while such atrocities happened in Whitechapel and reminded myself that this was why John was so careful to keep me from details of the cases he worked with you."

My head had sunk down upon my chest as I considered. Intelligent woman that she was, Mrs. Watson did not press me for my thoughts. Not immediately, anyhow. She rose from her couch. "If I may be so bold, I could permit you to see his study. On the chance that it might hold any clues as to the truth behind John's actions."

Leaping up, I beamed, "That would be most useful, yes. And I will, of course, be the one who dares violate the man's privacy so as to preserve for you your happy home. Lead away, Mrs. Watson."

Together we went to Watson's study. Mary waited patiently to the side while I made my preliminary investigation.

Things appeared to be mostly in order, save for a bundle of very folded, terribly wrinkled clothing he had secured within an old black medical satchel— the mysterious wayward bag that he had left at the

City Mortuary. Had it only been a day ago? It seemed a lifetime.

Leaning close, I sniffed the contents and recoiled. Paraffin? How odd. I tried again, this time catching also the sour notes of blossoming mould. It would appear that the doctor had tried—poorly—to remove some sort of stain—blood?—from the clothing and then, giving up entirely, hid it away while the cloth was still damp.

Reaching up, I dragged the nearby lamp close so as not to disturb the satchel. The worn black leather divulged few secrets, preferring reserved reticence in answer to my whispered queries. Gingerly I lifted its edge and peered at the underside. Again, its aged face was seamed with the lines of many a call upon many a patient. It spoke of long tense hours, the occasional accident with this sharp instrument or that caustic element. Scrapes, knocks, and bumps had left their separate histories.

A-ha! One more stain caught my eye. Now I did have to bring the bag further into the light. Carefully turning the old black bag upon its side, I peered at the stiffened patch of leather. The stain—it could have been blood, it could have been any number of things—was dark, well set, and relatively fresh. Again, with the small perils of my friend's chosen profession, the presence of the stain was not particularly alarming. It was its shape that interested me.

Turning the bottom of the bag back towards the ground, I imagined how the rest of the spill would have looked. Closing my eyes, I could see the red stain, pooling upon the ground and reaching, reaching ever onwards towards the bag that had been hastily set down near its edge. Crimson met black and—

My eyes snapped open. Aware that I was breathing heavily and—I'll admit it here and now—shaking all over, I looked up to find that Mrs. Watson had gone, called away on some invisible and tactful errand. That or John had returned. I listened intently to the sounds of quiet domesticity for the length of three whole minutes. All was well. All save for a bloodstained bag stuffed with incriminating clothing in the private study of one John H. Watson.

I carefully replaced both lamp and satchel and continued my inspection of the room. Mrs. Watson returned before I could complete my attentions on John's bookshelves, which were cluttered with all manner of miscellany.

"Has he a memorandum-book? Something in which he might have dates and other patient information?" I asked my question through dry lips.

"If there is nothing laid out, then it would be locked within his desk." Mary gestured helplessly.

I knelt and eyed the lock.

"No matter," I murmured. "If you should wish to be wholly honest when you say that you had no part in the opening of John's desk, I suggest you turn the other way now."

The lady did not flinch, wonderful woman that she was.

The lock was simple, and within moments I was rifling through the contents of the doctor's desk. It yielded its prize readily.

Taking out the small book, I eagerly thumbed its pages. The minutes ticked past, a reminder that I ought to conclude my business here sooner rather than later lest Watson come home to my strange tête-à-tête with his wife. Dates snagged themselves on my memory. April 2nd, night of Mrs. Emma

117

Smith's murder. Monday, August 6th, date of Martha Tabram's demise. Two days that Watson had falsely claimed to be with me at Baker Street.

No!

Frantic, I paged forward. Friday, the 31st of August and Saturday, September 1st—a stretch containing Mary Ann Nichols' final hours on this earth. Friday, September 7th, date of Mrs. Annie Chapman's untimely death. And lastly, September 29th, witness to the unravelling of my trust of John Watson alongside two more gruesome murders and the latest in Watson's lies to his wife as to his whereabouts.

On each of these dates was marked the simple scrawled word: "Mary."

MRS. WATSON

CHAPTER 13

M ary.
My eyes refused to tear themselves from Watson's note-book, and my legs forced me into the desk chair. I took advantage of my helplessness and thumbed back through the book a second time, now looking for any other dates with the same cryptic inscription. Three more selfsame notations leapt off the page—two from early July and one from far back in March. If there had been Ripper murders those nights, they had been overlooked.

Five and fifteen more. Threat, clue, and dark promise.

"Sherlock . . ."

"Say nothing to John about this." I rose and faced her at last.

"And when he does come home? What shall I—?"

"Say nothing, do nothing that lets on what you now know. And I shall be doing the same."

"Oh, but, Sherlock!"

"If you love him, you must. John's liberty—nay, his life—may well depend upon your silence on this. All this, as well as your own happiness, hang upon him not suspecting that either you or I know of his deception these many months." I turned and replaced the book within the desk. A quick application of my lock-picks secured the drawer.

I could still feel her eyes upon me, quietly pleading. Misgiving and fear each made their separate arguments. She said, "To lie to him. Does that not make my actions as terrible as his? Does one lie truly compel another?"

"I know you can do this."

"I cannot."

"I have known very few whose abilities to retain both nerve and wit under pressure rival your own, Mrs. Watson. John has that quality. I could never have permitted dear Watson—" My voice betrayed me and broke upon the name. "I could not have hoped for a better partner for my friend. And that alone has me certain that, if he lies to you, he has good reason and holds the best intents at heart. Let him live in the safety of that lie a little longer so that I may secure his freedom from it through my own methods. Again if you love him—"

"I do!"

"As do I." With great effort I cut myself off from my emotions. A deep breath and I felt much more like myself. "Now. He cannot suspect. Let me be absolutely clear upon this point. He must not be made aware of your knowledge. In this way, I am certain he will continue going about his business. When he does, when he next claims to be staying with me at 221, then send me a telegram. Mrs. Hudson will not permit such a delicate communiqué to fall into the wrong hands. Summon me the second John repeats this deception."

"I understand."

"You are not alone in this, Mary. Remember that."

"I know. And thank you, Sherlock. From both John and I—thank you."

With Mary's words in my heart and John's damning dates within my note-book, I rode home to Baker Street. There I summoned the full force of my irregulars via Billy Wiggins. I explained the situation to him in couched terms: Watson was in trouble, pressed by some unseeable evil. In order to protect him, I needed Billy and his subordinates to ensure they had eyes upon the doctor at all times. Furthermore, in the event that any of the boys discovered they were followed or watched in any way, word was to be sent to me. No matter the hour. No matter the day. I needed information. As an afterthought, and with a pang in my chest, I added—and Mary Watson, too.

God only knew how deep the danger ran. And from what direction.

Meeting concluded, I locked myself in my rooms and refused all comers. I am certain that, during that dark afternoon, Mrs. Hudson beat upon my door with a force both wholly concerned and nigh on desperate. Lost to my thoughts, I heard nothing of it. For nothing could ring louder than the condemning peal of the evidence I had discovered in Dr. Watson's desk and through his wife's unwitting testimony. My dearest friend in all the world not only resembled the cruellest killer in London's history in every particular, but he had confirmed, in his own hand, that he had lied as to his whereabouts on the nights of every murder for which he was a suspect.

My hope—my fear—was that I might scour my index for murder done on those other three unconsidered dates and find nothing for my efforts. For at this perilous juncture in my case, I could not take solace in a damning clue that led nowhere.

Thus I stayed, the modern Prometheus, until the day had given itself over to night.

FUNERAL IN WHITECHAPEL

CHAPTER 14

Eventually I deigned to unsecure my door and allow my landlady to present her well-earned scolding of my behaviour. The newspaper gave me the date. Mrs. Hudson provided strong coffee, rashers and eggs, and a forced airing of the room. My pent-up tobacco cloud rushed from the sitting area in a relieved gasp.

"I don't care what case you're on, Mr. Holmes. The stakes be what they will, if you don't care for yourself, you'll be of no use to anyone."

"Thank you, Mrs. Hudson, for your kind ministrations," I tried my hand at politeness and found that it came as easily as any other role. This in spite of my racing, still-distracted brain.

"Scared me half to death with your sulking. I almost called Dr. Watson in to roust you."

This had me more alert. I affected a smile and moved to the breakfast table. "Unnecessary. But I thank you. It is, as you say, just another case. And one which has grown decidedly cold, unlike this excellent repast you've brought me."

Her pursed lips told me she was not at all taken in by my droll flattery, but she did leave me alone in the end. Setting aside my cup, I attacked the papers. Nothing, nothing, and more nothing.

I flung the pile to my feet and stewed.

Another summons drove me from my chair. It was Mrs. Hudson returned.

"Telegram for you, Sherlock."

I charged at it same as I had the news. It read:

MAY BE NOTHING BUT HE IS GONE STOP MARY

I was dressed and out the door before Mrs. Hudson could voice to me her lamentation that I had neglected, once more, to sit down for a proper meal. I had left with her, however, a hasty plea to have Watson wait for my return should he arrive while I was gone.

I arrived at the Watson residence and alighted the steps in one terrific bound. The wholesome calm of the building had gone, and in its place now stood a tremulous expectation. My harsh ringing of the bell did nothing to improve the situation, and I entered to find Mrs. Watson all aflutter with nerves, flanked by a wan-faced servant.

"I'll be fine, Julie," she whispered, gesturing that I sit.

But the tension would not leave my limbs so easily. I moved to stand before the opened window. Standing became pacing, my eyes never leaving that broad square of glass and the scene beyond. Like a tiger at Regent's Zoo, I strained at my confines, my nostrils quivering each time I passed through the small breeze the portal ushered into the room, until a gentle noise from Mrs. Watson allowed me to realize, at last, that my movements were distressing her further. I sat. Reluctant but obedient.

Dr. Watson had told his wife that he had gone to Baker Street. We would soon know the extent of the truth to his claim. I cast my eyes to Mary, reading her emotional state in her body language, in the manner of dress she had adopted for the day. Outwardly calm, she was falling apart on the inside. But then, so was I—in my own way.

She startled, and I followed her surprised line of sight to the glass behind me.

A boy stood outside, furtive and nervously looking around lest his actions be noted by someone of the constabulary persuasion. He was, of course, one of my Baker Street irregulars. I rose and held hushed conference by the open window. "You have not been followed? You're certain? Good."

The report came that Dr. John Watson had apparently gone to Baker Street, rendering his statement to Mary true, for once. Thanking my man and passing him his coin, I straightened and updated my host on the particulars. Taking my leave, I then returned to Baker Street only to find there that I had just missed Watson. He had left behind his apologies with Mrs. Hudson and the curt explanation that he had been pressed for time. Watson had, apparently, come calling as there was a patient he had needed to see to in my neighbourhood.

Freshly annoyed by these developments and my wild chase for nothing, I sat and waited for word from my boys. In time it was reported to me via Wiggins that Watson, indeed, appeared to have visited a patient two blocks over before later returning home.

Thus I repeated my ritual of locking the door to my rooms and submerging my brain in cold coffee—I hadn't the heart to ring Mrs. Hudson for fresh—

and strong tobacco. More time passed, a steady alternation of day and night punctuated by the regular delivery of newspaper sheaves as well as a solitary note from Lestrade: "Nothing new to report. All was quiet in Whitechapel, thank God."

All remained quiet within 221B Baker Street, too, until—

"Holmes! It is Watson." The knocking at my door came more polite than I had any right to expect. I blinked my haze of brainwork from my vision and rose to answer the summons.

Both Mrs. Hudson and Dr. Watson practically tumbled into the room.

"Good heavens, Holmes. What a poisonous fog you've managed to secure."

Without a word to me, Mrs. Hudson merely placed upon the table a large dinner—enough for five men. As she exited, she passed a look to Watson, one I knew all too well and confirmed by the doctor's answering nod: See that he eats.

"Did she beg your presence here?" I asked, surrendering to the meal.

Watson sat himself opposite, his face troubled in spite of my attempts at dark levity. "Would it matter, Holmes?"

"What day is it?" I eyed the tangle that had piled itself up round my feet, an uneven snowfall of newsprint. I had read them all, sure. But, too, I had forgot most of it as immaterial.

He frowned and shifted in his chair uneasily. "It is October the 8th and it is a Monday."

I glanced at my watch. "Half past nine. Too soon for dinner."

"Really, Holmes." Watson stopped himself shy of saying more. Together we took up a quiet, affable but tense, meal. At length my companion ventured, "The funeral for Catherine Eddowes is this afternoon at one o'clock. I had thought I might pay my respects and that you might accompany me."

"Eddowes. The Mitre Square victim." What the devil was I to be there for? My keen interest roused, I gave a simple nod of acquiescence.

Watson beamed at me. "Excellent. I was half afraid I would be refused. You need to get out, Holmes. You need to stir from that couch and that pipe."

"And remind myself more fully of the case upon which I am embroiled?" I raised a sardonic eyebrow to the doctor's reasoning. "You are, of course, correct. I've been buried in data. I need to reconnect with the human element of this puzzle."

That he did not correct my callously calling this series of tragedies a "puzzle" spoke to his endless patience with me. This patience was further tested when he allowed me to make us both up so that we would better blend in with the populace of London's East End. Within the hour we were off in a hansom to Whitechapel, Watson's eyes fixed on the road ahead and mine slyly stealing to his face as much as I dared. My conclusion that this interlude should prove interesting, if not illuminating, rang 'round in my head for the duration of our journey eastward to Commercial Road.

With the pungent air of late-morning London assaulting my nose, I concurred with Watson's aim to drag me from my den and out into the world. That our errand was to conclude with a funeral kept my mind from soaring off into parts unknown. Still, the city infected my blood, its curious pathology growing within me that fever to which I had always had such easy susceptibility. I found that I hummed a light, staccato little aire as we bumped along.

For days I had been forced to retread old ground, grinding my mental powers on an unyielding millstone. Perhaps this would give me something at last. Faces to watch; time with Watson to think, to reconsider my terrible doubts.

I had directed our driver to take the southmost path to our destination, aware that the crowds might be gathering in force along the path the funeral party was to take. We were headed for a community in mourning, a neighbourhood on edge having suffered blow after blow over many a month. Their grief was communal, their pain raw. The police anticipated a potential demonstration and had taken precautions. Watson and I were outsiders in the full.

Save for our connexions to the Ripper's case. The case that plagued my mind and heavied my heart. Inwardly I again thanked Watson for the forced excursion, for it allowed me renewed insight into his emotional state. For the face of he at whose side I sat was a man as haunted as myself. He still read as guilty to my eyes. Various muscle twitches, the manner in which he darted his gaze about and upon which it rested—all told of a soul-devouring anxiety. Men, women, policemen, young lads, and roustabouts, affluent and poor alike, all received the same mix of despair and suspicion from him. It was like gazing upon myself when the fire of my work was upon me.

Could it be that his presence at Mitre Square, his untruths to Mary, point to something so innocent as a desire to work my methods on his own? Watson had never been deaf to the call to heroism. Perhaps he had opted to follow the East End murders long before I had been engaged, before, even, he had come to caution me against involvement.

But the dates in his desk book! How could he know, in advance, of the Ripper's plans to strike?

With a groan, I leaned back into the bench and raised my hand to my face. An error of the greatest magnitude had struck my mind. A gross negligence of duty whose remedying would have to wait until my afternoon adventure with Watson had run its course.

In my haste and horror within Watson's study, I had neglected to look forward in his calendar. So caught up was I in the need to exonerate him of my suspicions, that the mere confirmation of my deepest fears had led me to overlook my most useful clue. I had to go back. And with the greatest haste possible.

"Thank you, Holmes," Watson's voice broke in on my thoughts.

I swivelled bleak eyes his way. He did not appear to have noticed my agitation. Unheard of. Nerves thrumming, we both exited our cab and joined the growing crowd along Whitechapel Road. I looked about, remembering my last mad dash down the wide corridor. I saw the narrow side street which had brought Lestrade and me to the sight of that night's first murder. Swivelling my head, I followed the hurried path our cab had taken westward to the scene of the second. In my mind's eye I pictured a furtive black-clad figure creeping through the shadows. A man with a black medical bag and moustache, and wearing a long black coat and low-pulled hat. Remembering the indications in the suspect's footprints, I added a limp to my imaginings. A limp, yes, but no lessening of speed. Our Jack was a hasty fellow, capable of doing much mischief in little time.

Movement close by my side drew my eye. Watson had removed the shabby cap I had clapped upon him before we had left Baker Street. The mourning party had turned the corner from Commercial Street not two blocks up. Around us, every head was bared. Various murmurs, snatches of prayer, whispered into the air. Save for that, silent and motionless, the throng waited for the funeral to pass by. The city held its breath and shed a tear for the open hearse as it rumbled past. A burnished coffin sat up top, its golden wood shining in the watery light of the afternoon sun. Behind it trailed the mourning coach with its sombre occupants.

The bereaved party continued on up the street. In its wake, the crowd dissolved in stages, a spell broken. I replaced my own hat and looked to my companion. Removing his handkerchief from his sleeve, Watson turned from me and busied himself in a loud blowing of his nose.

"Come, Watson," I beckoned. "Mrs. Hudson will want to feed us again. And I've stronger stuff for the spirit."

Nodding, he moved to follow. The corners of his eyes sparkled, and I spoke of various topics unrelated to our task so as to spare him the shame of his feelings. When at last he left Baker Street, it was to return home. And so I remained behind with nothing for myself to do save wait for word that he had, again, been called out on an errand so that I might spy upon my friend's personal affairs.

AN EXERCISE IN FUTILITY

CHAPTER 15

Watson did not leave his home for two days, a fact confirmed both by the lack of word from Mrs. Watson and the reports of my own boys in the street. It also appeared that the incident of the spy upon my spies had been an isolated event. That or the opposing side had become more crafty since the accosting of one of their own. Wiggins and his crew reported no further interference, and I, myself, enjoyed one uneventful sojourn past the Watson residence disguised as a peddler. (Uneventful, save for when an older lady made it her sworn duty to haggle me down on the price of a copper pot. I should have liked to retain that particular prop in my wardrobe but as the handle was loose, I might be able to reclaim it amongst the rubbish in a week's time.) I had begun to think I had stupidly followed the wrong trail when, again, the doctor was called away to a patient's side.

Mrs. Watson met me with some surprise.

I kept my greetings short but polite. "I'm not

certain as to how long away he will be this time as I am told he is out on a medical errand. But if you could make the back door available to me in the event we are surprised, I would be quite grateful. Now, if I might again inspect John's study, I believe I may clear our matter up in scant minutes' time."

Wordless and wide-eyed, Mrs. Watson pointed the way and moved to follow. Her anxiety painted the walls of our short walk, and I had half a mind to turn and pat her hand soothingly. I did not. The woman was of stern stuff. And, if right, I would soon have addressed the worst part of my suspicions. As to the lesser of my concerns . . . Well, if another woman was involved, I did not easily give false assurances. That topic was something I would rather confront John with upon our own time.

Watson's study looked just as I had left it. The same hard-to-break bachelor-like mess occupied the small table by the window-side armchair. Cold tea dredges and spent pipe; an overturned volume of a medical journal. Carefully, I lifted the periodical and inspected the article it lay open upon. *The Relief of the Morphia Craving by Sparteine and Nitro-glycerine.* Oscar Jennings, M. D., M.R.C.S., June 25, 1887 issue. Hardly instructive. I noted it and moved on.

Producing my lens, I went over the whole grounds of the study. Again, Watson's neglected bag with its odiferous contents engaged my attentions. Though I could guess from the weight of it that the ruined items were still hid within, I performed a quick check of this fact. The guilty secret remained.

I moved on to the desk, no longer possessing even the slimmest of hopes.

My lock-picks knew the way, having trod these paths before. The memorandum-book opened to my tremoring fingers. My breath held, I paged to October 1888.

"Mary" scrawled in red ink. The 14th of October—but four days hence. I groaned and paged forward again. October 30th and another inscription of the same. Heart sinking, I continued my hellish pursuit for the truth. Both November 8th and 9th bore the mark. As did the 30th. December was yet clean.

With a sharp intake of breath, I copied down the dates and re-secured the book within Watson's desk. I exited the study to find a young woman clad in the sombre black and white of household staff hurrying down the hallway towards me. She beckoned me silently, and I saw that she had my hat and cane in hand. She said, "Mr. Holmes. Mrs. Watson sent me to find you and let you out through the kitchens. She has detained Dr. Watson at the front through some excuse."

I hurried to follow, and we managed to duck into the kitchens unseen. Here, with shining eyes of hope, she opened the door that led out back. "Thank you, Mr. Holmes."

My returned smile was fleeting, but I managed it. I turned to the small yard, estimating the effort it would take to leverage myself out into the mews that stood not twenty paces off—behind a fence and between two close-pressed buildings. Neither easy nor impossible. Nor had I much choice.

The maid's hand on my arm stopped me. She pointed. "That slat there, the discoloured one. It's the easiest hand up. Though the two next to it are a touch loose and aren't to be trusted. Same with the drain pipe beyond. There's three bricks shifted outward a bit and with your height, you'll find an easier time of it than—" She stopped, blushing.

I turned fully to regard the young woman at my side, setting stern eyes upon her but allowing my mouth to twitch with ill-concealed mirth. I offered, "My friend keeps a conservative house, but he is a romantic at heart. The next time your gentleman comes calling, he should ask that he be let in at the front of the house rather than risk his limbs over so unusual an entrance."

Scant minutes later, with a new scuff on my right shoe and a new plan for the case within my heart, I ran southbound through the Eastbourne mews. Returning to my rooms at Baker Street, I wondered, again, how well I actually knew my friend. Of the three observations within Watson's study that had caught my attention, two had surprised me.

The one, the most pressing, was that of the dates within his date book. The appointments rang both damning and peculiarly innocent to my mind. This latter instinct I considered no more helpful than hope. Consequently, having expected to find what I had within the pages of his memorandum-book, I had remained unsurprised by the revelation.

The bag of musty clothes with the stain on its underside? That could be explained away by my friend's profession. I had approached with a mind bent towards the macabre and subsequently read the evidence in that light. My surprise in the discovery came from the bag still being there at all. Watson's respect for his calling was matched only by his atten-tion to detail in his practice of it. That the black medical bag should be so neglected spoke to either a distracted mind or a guilty conscience.

Lastly, however, came the fact which had

momentarily made me question, not only the past several months of Watson's activities, but years. In checking over his study for this second time, I had found next to no written evidence of our partnership. This from a man who had taken meticulous notes on our cases and who had turned those notes into, admittedly purple, prose. Where had it all gone? Surely, if he had another study or place in which he worked, Mrs. Watson would have shown it to me. Additionally, his stores were not entirely barren. Several copies of *Beeton's* had been stowed upon the shelves and in drawers. There, too, had been a few—very few—note-books, sketches of cases but nothing substantial.

Someone had Watson's stories. Someone was reading them and making terrible use of what he learned. I breathed a sigh of relief, believing that I, again, had two cases rather than the one. My renewed confidence led me to make the following list:

Doctor John H. Watson, a puzzle.

1. ~~Enemies~~— *None!*

This first item writ and scratched out and then peevishly re-added down below with the following addendum:

1. Enemies – My enemies, then. Those of S. H. and the Law itself.

For it could still well be that this game was being played against myself.

2. Other threats.

Admirers

~~Family trouble~~

Again, with no family, I could safely close this

door. By Watson's own admission at the outset of the Morstan case, his brother had passed away the year before. John had become the recipient of his father's watch then, and his marriage the previous fall had brought no other Watsons 'round for the happy occasion.

And yet Watson's private worries and furtive actions seemed, to me, not those of a man under the threat from an outside force. My list continued:

3. Financial?*

I considered the number of times Watson's check book had sat secured within my desk, and how often he had proved unskilled in the area of predicting a horse's speed on the field. This bore consideration. I made a small mark with my pencil, a reminder to return to this note for further thought.

4. Health.

Preposterous. I let it stand, however. While not clearly ill, he did not seem altogether well.

5. Professional?*

Again, where had all his manuscripts gone? Another mark of my pencil gave this point priority.

6. A romantic entang—

This I didn't bother to complete. Preposterous!

But then, was it not also preposterous that I could have thought Watson to be Jack the Ripper? And who was this "Mary" in Watson's date book if not his wife, she who claimed him absent from home —and with me!—each of the nights in question.

I moved on.

Beneath it, I penned a second column.

Lies the Ripper has told:
   1. "Five. And fifteen more."

The fifth? Still undiscovered. This, if I allowed Emma Smith to be counted amongst the Ripper's victims as Watson had once suggested. I had scoured the news, asked my questions of the police, made my own private inquiries. Therefore I assumed the claim false, else in his vanity the Ripper would have ensured that we knew of this missing victim.

2. "Ears."

Utter tosh. A gibe at me. But telling of what he knew and at what game he was playing.

3. Handwriting and education

A misdirect in every particular save for, perhaps, height.

4. Goulston Street's chalked graffiti.

Upon this point I was forced to venture into guesswork—horrid thought—as I had not seen it firsthand. But I believed it a red herring, something to stir the public sentiment and throw the police upon the wrong scent.

5. Disguise?

This held water. How else might our man have slipped through the tight net of the police every time? With his level of education and relatively well-drawn profile from witness accounts, he had to be doing something to conceal his fleeing of the scene.

That or he went to ground.

6. Bolt-hole – *How to discover?*

By week's end I hoped I would have the answer to at least one, if not more, of these questions.

Four days later found me with many more miles underfoot. I had been to the Central News Agency. I had also visited the offices of Ward Lock & Co over on Paternoster Row. Finding myself a stone's throw from the Central Criminal Court, I called there, too, just so that I might refresh myself with the scent of villainy that could be solved.

Lastly, I checked in with Lestrade and told him I had made no progress whatsoever on the Ripper case. I'm not all that certain he believed me.

In the end, I had a working list of new considerations. Anyone who would have thumbed through Watson's work had earned himself a spot upon it. The creation of this file of suspects was no mean task, considering the tight-lipped nature of the business and my outsider status. I had not gone as myself, of course—his publishers, I believe, considered me to be purely fictional—but had instead made up a rather elaborate backstory of familial connexion for Watson's *nom de plume*. Forwarding the story of a mislaid manuscript, one the author was eager to have back or at least know of its whereabouts, I thus began a wild roundabout series of tailings and conversations.

Some of it was sure to get back to Watson, I knew, in spite of my cautions. Well, then, let that be the case. I had needed leads other than him. I now had several. Tenuous and circumstantial, sure. But so many men had things in their lives, vices and weaknesses which could eat at a person like a cancer, that one solid clue might prove the final unravelling of the ugly knot that lay tangled within my fist.

I could only pray the two threads were connected as they appeared and that I was, at last, ahead of our Ripper.

Seven. And thirteen more. I must move fast.

A TELEGRAM AND A DARK VIGIL

CHAPTER 16

Dusk had fallen, and a sickly yellow fog had begun to press against the panes of 221B Baker Street before Mrs. Watson's telegram reached me on the evening of October 14th. I had spent the afternoon in the grips of tense unease, worried I had made the wrong decision for the night's plans. If the Ripper were to strike while I had sat silent upon new and key information in the case . . . But, no. No matter which way I looked at it, I had found no justification for bringing Lestrade in. What I had was coincidence. At least that is what I told myself as I rode the dark, dun-coloured streets. And I firmly disbelieved in coincidence.

Watson's date book was his own business, and I was determined to keep it that way as long as I dare.

HE IS GONE STOP COME AT ONCE STOP MARY

And so I came at once.

And so I had loosed my hounds upon the quiet city, a pack of eager children intent on little more than adventure and a guinea to the first to find their quarry and bring word back to me. The telegram itself now lay within the grate of 221b's hearth, an immolation to London's night skies.

Traffic slowed at Bishop's Road Bridge, prompting an impatient rap from me. I disembarked early and walked the rest of the short journey. I required somewhere to pour off my energies, and the ochre mist parted before my long strides like a curtain. Ahead, the Watson home shone like a beacon. I hurried my steps and was admitted to the warm and inviting sitting room by the lady of the house herself.

She appeared well under her obvious strain. Her eyes bright, her face drawn but steady, only Mary's hands betrayed a tremor of fear as she rang for the servant. With whispered words, she confirmed for me that Watson had told her he expected to stay the night at Baker Street.

Coffee and stronger stuffs were produced, and the two of us settled in for what was to be a potentially lengthy vigil, Mrs. Watson by the fire with a book she did not read, and I by my window with a pipe I did not smoke. Neither of us spoke, with the drawn silence broken only by the crackle of logs shifting in the grate, the soft ticking of a clock, and the occasional rumble of fitful traffic on the street outside.

My discomfort grew irksome as the night aged. I did not mind a non-loquacious quiet. John could testify to that. But I was increasingly aware of my outsider status as I sat by the window, waiting for report of my friend's activities. I sat in Watson's chair on a Sunday evening. Watson's chair with Watson's wife in Watson's house. The strange intimacy of it all nearly forced me to my feet. But, no, were I to abandon my post, I might miss the report from my informants and thus throw the whole scheme into error. I sat and I stewed, chewing the end of my pipe thoughtfully.

Watson has claimed that, when on a case, I tend to eschew food and drink, that I do not require sleep. True, the energies of my work tend to spur me more than the baser stuffs upon which human existence depends. However, during that interminable wait at the Watson home, I found my eyes drooping and my head nodding. I blame the tension of the whole. It would break a lesser man, and I am not ashamed of the utter exhaustion to which it drove me while I sat within the cozy comforts of my friend's home.

At length, movement in the other end of the room drew my eye, and I turned, senses sharpened. Mrs. Watson had risen to her feet. "I'm sorry, Mr. Holmes, but I must see to drawing the curtains. The hour being as late as it is, I fear that even our extraordinary circumstances do not excuse subjecting ourselves to the sort of commentary from the neighbours this watchfulness is sure to provoke."

I smiled and moved to assist. I only needed but the smallest sliver from which to continue my wait, and in compromise I was allowed to open the window a little. We both retook our places as the nearby church bells rang out a haunting ten o'clock chime. The cool damp of the night air breezing over my face did much to refresh me, and I was able to resume my vigil with less irritation than before.

I had begun to think our attentions something of a fool's errand when rustling in the vegetation near the window caught my eyes and ears. Moving forward I crouched to hold whispered conference with my man, Wiggins himself. He received his guinea with solemn earnestness and then told me where in the city Watson had stopped off. Billy had left a boy behind, lest the doctor move on from his perch. When the address of the building reached my ears I drew back in surprise.

"You're certain?" I asked.

"Sure as I am of my own name," he replied and then waited for further instructions.

These were for him to go home. He had done a good night's work and had left more than enough agents in the field. The task was now upon myself to complete.

Shutting the window and drawing the curtain its last inch, I turned to find Mrs. Watson eagerly awaiting word. I will confess that I do not remember all of what I said to her that night. I recall half-hearted attempts at comfort, hasty ill-conceived explanations which left me cold. And then I was off to hail as fast a cab as I might.

My destination: eastward through London's East End to 37 Mary Street.

The dates in Watson's journal were not in reference to a woman, then. Smiling grimly to myself within the swaying hansom, I considered the list I had compiled earlier in the week. Soon I would have the answer to at least one of my most pressing questions. I could only pray they were all as innocently resolved as this first.

Whitechapel passed me by in a golden-hued blur, the disheartening weather pooling beneath gaslights so as to soften its grief-hardened edges. The low-hanging clouds had wrapped the district in a blanket of solace, and the light refracting through the various street lamps seemed to render the dark corners brighter than their wont. While some might think London's fog an aid to the criminal element, I found that the slowing of foot traffic and greater vigilance of the populace often led to a dampening of murder and burglary. A fleeing fugitive always had better luck of it when his way was clear and his eyes undimmed.

At length, my driver turned onto Harley Street, and I rapped my instructions that I should like to disembark. The thickening weather was to render my search for house numbers more difficult, but I valued caution over expediency at this point. I made for the intersection of Mary Street and stuck to the shadows as best I could. At this late hour, it being a Sunday night—or had we already crossed into Monday morning?—the street was vacant and oppressively silent. A few lights burned behind heavily curtained windows, but even in the heavy fog, the house at the top of the street caught my eye. There several lamps blazed, and the shades had been imperfectly drawn. Still, there was little to see. The ground floor, while handsomely appointed, carried within it a shabby but prideful attitude. And was decidedly empty of people in spite of its illumination. The upper storey—that would prove more difficult. Casting a furtive glance around, I considered the tree out front and then eyed the drain pipe on the corner. Neither seemed conducive to my purposes. And as the situation did not yet seem alarming so much as merely puzzling in the eyes of the law, I did not wish to put myself in so awkward a position. I chose, instead, to read the front walk by the light of my pocket lantern. Whipping out my lens, I bent close. The wetness of the evening had preserved many of the tell-tale marks of passersby. I could see in an instant that one man had entered the house and no one had left it. I could tell, too, where the individual had disembarked from his cab. The gait pronounced a man of a little over five and a half feet, in good training, but not altogether thin. Had I not been able to recognise my Watson in this evidence, the presence of a spent cigarette stub on the sidewalk confirmed it for me. "Bradley, Oxford Street" read the stamp on its end. I pocketed the evidence and moved to retrace my steps back up the path when suddenly the door opened.

My choice in that instant was to leap to the side and pray I had not been seen—a ridiculous notion— or confront Dr. John H. Watson then and there. For it was he who now stood upon the stoop of the mysterious Mary Street residence and he who paused agog to stare at the man who crouched not ten paces from him, strong lens in hand and guilt upon his face.

The doctor frowned, taking in my unexpected appearance with measured calm. He seemed to be debating within himself whether to give greeting and pretend something akin to normalcy or fly back within the confines of the house and lock the door behind him. With me, the former was the wiser move and this is what he now chose.

"Why, Holmes, whatever brings you to this lonesome place at such a late hour?" he began, coming up the path towards me so that he might keep his greeting quiet.

I took in the various details of his dress and posture, making my conclusions. It drew my anger that he could be so cool, but I managed my own measured, "I should ask the same of you, Watson."

He paused, assessing me as I had him. My ire became his. "I——! I don't have to answer to you, Holmes."

"No. But you should tell the truth to your wife. Seeing as she believes you are currently with me at Baker Street."

"My wife!" he sputtered. "You don't mean to say —? How dare you! How dare you, Holmes! What I get up to in my work is my business—"

"You mean to have me think that you are here on medical business, Watson?" Fire met fire, and I sprang upon him with my words. "Looking as you do. Please. Do remember that I am not a fool. And if you are going to continue on in this fashion, I would ask that you leave me and 221B out of this!"

"That will certainly not be a problem. I— Where are you going?"

I had brushed past him while he spoke, angrily intent on the door. Watson inserted himself none too gently between me and the darkened portal. "Absolutely not! I cannot allow this, Holmes. Are you mad, man? This is not one of your cases where you can simply elect to take justice into your own hands and — Oh, my goodness, you—!"

I stood back and met his outburst with cold calm. "I, what, Watson?"

He stared, amazed. "I am one of your cases. Aren't I? Damn you, Holmes. Which is it then? Am I the suspect? Or maybe you're reserving that honour for the poor invalid inside this home. What happens if I cry for the police, are they on your side or mine? Are you in the right or am I?"

I made no response but still stood regarding him with measured calm. I would not let on to him how much of an utter disaster my case had just become. To raise a scene? Again I still held on to faint hope that I might yet save him from . . . from whatever black business he had become enmeshed. He seemed to sense my disinclination to rush headlong into the home behind him, and he relaxed, if only slightly.

"Go home, Holmes. You've no business here." Watson's jaw clenched as he said the words, and I could feel him tense, subtle and silent assurance that he was ready for whatever was to come next from me, that he would resist on every particular until either he or I had fallen.

And so I did the unexpected. I left. I returned to Baker Street and pursued my own business concluding that, if his work and mine were on a course for sure collision, then so be it.

FROM HELL

CHAPTER 17

Two days later, the following letter sat upon my desk, and Inspector Lestrade of Scotland Yard sat within the cane chair which occupied the sitting room at 221B Baker Street. The short missive was addressed to Mr. George Lusk, leader of the Whitechapel Vigilance Committee, and had been postmarked that morning "From Hell."

Mr Lusk,
  Sir
  I send you half the Kidne I took from one women preserved it for you tother piece I fried and ate it was very nice. I may send you the bloody knife that took it out if you only wate a while longer
  signed
  Catch me when you can Mishter Lusk

Accompanying this remarkable communication had

been a small box containing half a kidney preserved in wine. This key piece of evidence had not made its way into my hands but had, instead, gone to the medical authorities in the case. I was told that they were even now determining whether the organ belonged to any of the Ripper's victims.

"He almost did not bring this forward, so assured was he that it was all an elaborate hoax," Lestrade explained again, desperate to fill the silence between us.

I could think and observe all at once and replied, "Why Mr. Lusk? He is an unusual person to have received such a communication. Why would our man not contact the press again? Or the police? Why change his game now?"

"After the papers printed that first missive we've been drowning in letters purportedly from the Ripper himself, and I think he, Jack, knows it." Lestrade shook his head. "And Mr. Lusk has been under quiet surveillance by our force since his having been elected chairman of the Vigilance Committee last month has put him ill at ease over his safety."

"The Ripper kills women who sell themselves, not middle-aged businessmen who would like their neighbourhood free of brutal murders," I quipped then blanched. "Apologies. But I do not understand why this killer would elect so sudden a change save for if he's desperate, as this letter seems to read. But why? Why should he feel pressed unless the police and this so-called Vigilance Committee have managed to foil one of his attempts at outrage?"

"There you have it, Mr. Holmes!" Lestrade crowed, triumphant. "Now if we only could determine what it was that we had done right, we might have him!"

"Yes, if only," I mused, thoughtful. My young informants had, indeed, reported back that Watson had gone immediately home to James Street following our confrontation on the night of the 14th.

My subsequent round-the-clock watch on the Mary Street house had reported no change since. My urchins would beggar me before the new year, and my irregulars would be rich as kings should this case not let up, and soon. Ah, but then we still had October 30th to look forward to.

The simple fact remained: Watson had been forced to alter his plans this week, and immediately after? Clear anxiety from our Jack.

I scowled, rising. "Shall we visit the doctor and see what he has to tell of the kidney's origins? I believe I have all I can glean from this letter. The Ripper is eager to remain prominent in our minds. Also he is maintaining the charade of ill-education— note his atrocious spelling but the fact that he has somehow managed to keep the silent 'k' in 'knife' and 'h' in 'while,' Inspector. I've no doubt he'll strike again some day very soon."

Together we rode to Scotland Yard, the planned rendezvous for all data related to the Ripper case. Doctor Brown met us there, bringing with him the grisly evidence to surrender back to the detectives on the case. It was his opinion that the kidney might well be a match to Catherine Eddowes but, as the deceased had already been buried, there was no easy way to confirm this.

"And do you believe there a chance this specimen could have come from say, a laboratory? Could this be a hoax by some medical student?" I pressed, already knowing the answer, having made cursory investigations over the box and its contents while the doctor had spoken.

"No, sir. I do not," Dr. Brown sniffed disdainfully. "Wine, as you know, is not a typical preserver of medical organs. And the kidney is not charged with the fluids one would find in dissection rooms. If not Eddowes' kidney, this was illegally obtained from some other body."

With that, the doctor left, and we resumed our reconsiderations of fact.

"Well, Holmes, I suppose we ought to add to our list of suspects all medical students and those working in or near hospitals and mortuaries to go along with men who read the daily paper," Lestrade grumbled and collapsed into a chair.

"Now, now," I cautioned, "Do not fall to the error of despair. You can safely eliminate all those who fall outside the physical description given by the witnesses, leaving us a much narrower field to comb."

He eyed me with disgust then lapsed into a small smile. "We foiled him though, didn't we?"

"That we may have, yes." I reached for the letter once again. "And we will yet again."

"But when, Holmes?" he cried.

My conscience twinged. Not meeting his gaze, I offered, "I would suggest extra vigilance upon the night of October 30th."

He was not put off. The detective rose and peered over my elbow at the letter in my hand. "And why's that, Mr. Holmes?"

I replaced the letter upon the desk and turned to him, cold calculating machine to the fullest. "Jack has had a quiet month. He'll want the furore of this latest missive to catch in the public's mind and drive them to greater fear and action. His past history suggests that he favours the end of the month as well as the first third. We will be deep within a waning crescent then, giving him the cover he prefers for his dark deeds. Mark my word, Lestrade, the Ripper will strike on October 30th."

I had the distinct impression that he wished to ask more of me in that moment. But the Scotland Yard man stayed mute.

I made my way home via the vastly circuitous route of Whitechapel, and there I remained save for when I found excuse to follow this man or that upon my own list of suspects. With every crossing off of a name, new guilt sprang into my breast, guilt that I was hiding my side investigation from the police. And remorse that, with each elimination of a potential outside of Watson himself, I was drawing nearer to the unthinkable conclusion which I had, so far, striven to avoid.

Thus it was on the evening of October 30th that nothing whatsoever happened in the way of murder in Whitechapel. Nor did anything occur the day after.

I, myself, was not present for the non-events save as recipient of annoyed and triumphant communiqués from Inspector Lestrade on the matter. He and his men had walked every inch of the district for two nights and all for naught.

I wanted to remind him that no women were dead. Surely that was progress enough.

But he was right in that these efforts could not become permanent. We needed to catch Jack the Ripper, not merely foil his plans by making his hunting grounds inhospitable.

As for me, I had waited at home for a telegram

from Mrs. Watson that had never come. John had never left the house as he had intended. Therefore, no seemingly-unconnected tragedy had struck the East End. What did this portend?

I soon found out.

THE ENDING OF A FRIENDSHIP

CHAPTER 18

Aharsh ring upon 221's bell stirred me from my couch early on the morning of November 1st. I looked out to see a cab waiting in the street below. Hurried footsteps clamoured up the stairs and towards the door of my apartments. I only had time to smooth my hair and draw my blue dressing gown about my frame when the door burst open.

Watson invaded his former sanctuary, his eyes alight with anger. He quivered animatedly as he stood upon the carpet and declared, "There are police outside my house, Holmes. And I demand to know why!"

I had thought that nothing he could say to me would surprise me at this point in our frayed relationship. That he had come calling at all was, of course, unexpected. But to level such a claim and at me? I sat, as stunned by the veiled accusation as by the news.

"I have not the faintest idea why."

"You deny it then?" Further incensed by my claim of ignorance, he stamped his cane upon the floor and proceeded to dart his eyes about the room, as if seeking more profitable release for his energies. I heard Mrs. Hudson's rustling about on the landing and could imagine her anxiety over the extraordinary outburst.

"I do deny it, yes. You know how I tend to go about my investigations—"

"A-ha!" His voice crescendoed with the word. "So you do admit that you have me under your microscope. You and your—" he sputtered and tried again, "You and your cold, disaffected logic."

He turned around, moving as if to leave. He turned back, "Well, I'll have you know that by your unfounded suspicions you have utterly upset my wife, completely ruined what friendship we had left, and made a terrific fool of yourself, Holmes. Would you believe that Mary would not let me out of the house the last two nights? Afraid for me, she is. And so my patients are left without their physician. The police? They can watch my house until Christmas comes. They can stand out in the cold and stare at my unmoving front door as long as they would like. Same as with Mary Street. You and that ridiculous Lestrade. You—you can have each other!"

And with that, he stormed back out of Baker Street and back out of my life.

I would have followed. I would have, truly, but for poor Mrs. Hudson huddling in a near faint upon the stairs. Under my careful ministrations, 221's landlady came round to herself, but she remained terribly upset for the remainder of the morning. None of my attempts at excusing Watson's behaviour swayed her. At one point, my wilting explanations earned me a mild reproof from her. "I'm not an idiot, Mr. Holmes, that you might think I can fall to such an obvious misrepresentation of what I myself heard and saw."

This was the second—or was it now the third?—time I had been accused thus by those whom I cared for most. I did not think either of them stupid. Far from it, else they would not have remained so instrumental to my life for so long as both Mrs. Hudson and John Watson had. But I was backed into the most irritating of corners and, quite simply, did not know how to behave in such circumstances. What was consolation but an unconvincing lie?

In the end, Mrs. Hudson's upset had waned enough by afternoon so that I was able to leave on an urgent errand of my own. I needed to have a word with detective Lestrade.

I confess that my entrance into Lestrade's offices at Scotland Yard was not much gentler than Watson's incursion into Baker Street had been. My wild eyes and energetic step were met with a pinched smile by the detective. Seated behind his desk, he gestured to the opposite chair and bade me sit. He then waited, forcing me to speak first and damn myself with my own line of impertinent questions, none least of which was, "Why is Dr. Watson's home being surveilled, Lestrade?"

"Why do you think, Mr. Holmes?"

His curl of the lip met with one of my own. Of all the sanctimonious, smug— I took a breath and focused my thoughts. Leaning back into my chair, I steepled my hands. "Other than for the potential that, through our investigation in the case, John, like

Mr. Lusk, has come up against threats to his safety and well-being, I cannot imagine any other possible reason. And I am hurt, Lestrade, that you did not think I merited such protection as well." I raised one sardonic eyebrow, gambit made.

He smiled, coldly. "Keep lying to yourself, Mr. Holmes. Continue on believing that your movements and those of your friend have never entered into our suspicions and that we poor, simple policemen cannot do a single thing without the aid of one Sherlock Holmes, consulting detective. Tell yourself that foolish old Lestrade and his ilk cannot see when you withhold evidence from them, giving them veiled hints and leads when suits your fancy. Go on and see that you don't push us into making an arrest in this Ripper case, proof in hand or not."

I could have been stone for all that his words moved me.

His smile widened, and he leaned forward over the desk. "Or perhaps you've the opposite? Some way to clear your friend's name?" Holding my gaze, he reached into a drawer and took out a small leather-bound memorandum-book. I darted my eyes to it and then back to the policeman's face. He noted the gesture and nodded his head in assent. "As you can see, we are not above a bit of the dirty to see that justice is served. Your friend needs to trust his household staff a little less. I trust that you've seen the date in his book? November 8th we make our move on *our* man. If you've a suspect of your own, I suggest you make arrangements for one of those grand little demonstrations of which you are so fond."

I rose. "Is that all, Lestrade?"

"Unless you've anything to add, Mr. Holmes."

"Good day to you then." I left, angrier than when I had come but infinitely more dangerous for it. This was one instance where the passions of high emotion could serve my mental faculties rather than act as the detractor. I had seven days. Let Lestrade see what I should do with them.

A LOCKED DOOR

CHAPTER 19

Six days later found me on the eve of November 7th. Much had been accomplished in that short, harried week, little of it good save for the warning I had dared to leave at the Watson residence. For that errand I had taken pains to come in disguise, counting a half a dozen of the constabulary persuasion on the street leading up to and away from the doctor's home. In their infinite wisdom, the police had not bothered to secure the surrounding streets nor the southmost entry of the mews. John was out, and Mrs. Watson had received my impassioned mandate with no small trepidation. I yet feared that she might not allow my instructions to be passed along. Never mind that, in coming from me, Watson might choose to ignore them entirely.

To Mary I had begged her not to interfere with her husband's goings on, should he elect to leave home on the 8th or 9th. My instructions for John were even more direct. For him I had a simple scrawled note: "If you must go to your patient, for God's sake, use the back door. S. H."

And then I waited, having but a dozen men left upon my list of potential suspects and twenty-four hours until Lestrade made his move against my friend. The hours grew intolerable, and I again gave myself over to smoking until I had reduced the atmosphere of 221b to something that even I found noxious and nigh unbreathable. It was a wonder Mrs. Hudson did not turn me out for once and for all.

Nighttime had darkened the windows when a ring upon the bell ushered in an urgent telegram.

HE HAS GONE STOP GODSPEED STOP MARY

I sent quick word through my irregulars that, if Watson were seen anywhere other than where I myself was headed—37 Mary Street—they should report his whereabouts to me at once. This came with a warning and reminder: the Watson residence was watched by the police. Baker Street, too, may have fallen under Lestrade's cautionary surveillance by now. See but do not be seen, that was their order.

I then made ready to leave. For this chase, I elected to be myself. I donned no disguise and made sure my revolver rode within the pocket of my long coat, a last-second precaution. The police likely knew of Mary Street. They likely knew everything. After all, I had accomplished so much already on my own—well, one man and a handful of ragamuffin street children. Surely Scotland Yard had set a watch upon the other place in which Watson had found refuge.

I arrived to find the cage empty, the bird flown.

Swearing softly to myself, I deftly avoided the attentions of the thin watch Lestrade had set upon 37 Mary Street. A swift application of my lockpicks

—there's a skill your men have need of, Lestrade!— and I was in.

Whoever had lived in and then abandoned this melancholy home had left in a hurry and, if I was not mistaken, much reluctance. Various bits of furniture lay strewn about, the larder practically barren. The man who had lived here had not lived well. The place was about as opposite the cheer of James Street as one could imagine. Cautious steps brought me up and into the living quarters, disused all, save for one bedroom overlooking the street. I remembered its placement within the whole, recalled how the light had shown through the shades as I stood in the lane below.

The bed had been recently occupied, but for how long I could only guess at, and this I refused to do. The closet, the side table, the dresser—all showed signs of recent occupancy by a man matching Watson's height and build, hair colour and temperament. The place had the air, the mood, of a sickroom, if not the particular odour of one. Judging myself safe enough from the lack of immediate interference, I opened my dark lantern and made further investigation of the dreary space. Its secrets opened themselves to me.

The manuscripts and case notes I had counted on as lost or misplaced by Watson? Sheaves of them lay about the room. I had, in several instances, whole cases which had been put to prose—ones he had not run by my eyes and, clearly, had not yet seen the pen of an editor. These, alongside half-formed scribbles, bespoke long hours hid away in this bleak place. The writing itself trembled with feeling, soared with angst, and grovelled in fear. I saw before me a transformation, a brief history of his guilt. My friend's hand had grown unsteady in the act of taking pen to paper, the heaviness of his terrible lie weighing even within his words.

I moved on. Hidden crevices, secure stores in floorboards and beneath drawers; the hollowed leg of the bed—each gave me something. In one, a collection of small glistening bottles; in another, a cunningly wrought case of maple, empty of the occupant that had once sat within its velvet lining. But the last yielded the truth:

A wicked needle and plunger.

It paired with the other paraphernalia to make a whole.

With hands that shook, I laid all out upon the bed, lest my shock shatter the evidence I had gathered at so high a cost. My mind reeled, repositioning my other data to make room for this new. The secret life Watson led was coming into greater focus, so sharp as to cut me upon its edges. My heart bled for my friend and the situation in which he had found himself. I knew full well what black fits came upon me when I resorted to such artificial stimulus and—in sniffing the contents of the glittering bottles—I knew he must be in greater danger than I ever had been, considering his constitution and the concentration of the chemicals found within. That he could have walked freely under the burden of so large a lie for as long as he must have was, to me, absolutely astonishing.

I wondered, could it be that Watson himself was unaware of his actions part of the time? The furtive guilt—I knew it well. The shame, this too, I had felt. As for the incredible depths of his grand deception? This I would confront when he returned from his nocturnal haunts, as surely he must. Any man held within the grip of a morphine addiction like as I had found here—one that led to these extraordinary measures of concealment—would require it. Again, this I should know having, to Watson's great concern, fallen to the drug's effects within his presence on more than one occasion during our partnership. Settling in on the floor by the bed, I waited for morning. A morning which came, went, and turned to night again. And all without producing Watson.

At length I rose and stretched and ransacked the kitchens for its awful leavings. Some stale bread and a bit of weak tea bolstered my constitution, and I was able to resume my vigil in the empty bedroom. Through the long day I never slept, my nerves as bright, as strained, as ever. I passed my time by reading his words, reliving our partnership as seen through Watson's eyes. Day gave over into night, and at long last, I had to admit to defeat. I could well wait here for a week and have nothing to show for it. And with Lestrade's trap threatening to close about Watson this very night? I might not know where my friend had spirited himself away to, but it wasn't altogether unreasonable to believe that, for once, Scotland Yard might know something Sherlock Holmes did not.

I waited in the darkness for as long as I dared and then stole out the way I had come.

Unkempt as I was, no cab would have me, and I was forced to hoof it westward into Spitalfields before my persona blended in enough to make me relatively respectable. From there I took a growler northward, somewhat imparticular in my direction save for a sudden whim to stop off at Ten Bells. I disembarked and made my way through the disaffected throng of a rainy Thursday night. The hour had grown late, and my curious glances at the strangers around me—none were Lestrade—had dwindled when at last I gave up this second unsuccessful vigil of my day.

Hailing a cab, I directed the driver towards home only to be accosted by the sharp scream of a police whistle and the cry of "Murder!"

At long last I freed myself to the case. I gave my name, widely and boldly, and the streets fell away before clattering hooves and sparking wheels. I soon reached the scene of the latest outrage, a small court, Miller's Court, off Dorset Street in one of the darkest, most dangerous parts of town—and a mere stone's throw from where I had spent the better part of my evening at Ten Bells.

Threading through the gathering crowd, I spotted the PC and again gave my name so as to clear a path. He pointed, not to the ground, but to a small lodging which opened on the corner of the yard. There a broken window showed a light within and a glimpse of a horror scarce to be conceived.

"Get them all back," I muttered, drawing forward and bending to peer through the missing glass. Taking out my lantern and lens, I inspected the steps leading to the door. By now the court's ground had been rendered useless by the various folks who had crossed and re-crossed the space. Even as I made my preliminary conclusions, two Yard officials came upon me as I worked. They introduced themselves.

Inspector Dew. Inspector Beck. Would Inspector Lestrade be joining us here? No, he would not.

This last came with—did I imagine?—a nervous glance between the two men. I continued my minute examinations of windowsill, door jamb, knob, lintel . . .

Inspector Beck moved to the window and peered in. He staggered back, crying out, "For God's sake, Dew! Don't look."

"Steady, man." I rose and fixed him with a stern eye. "Best you can do to help the woman now is to get ahold of yourself and do your job."

He gulped and nodded. In the light of both lantern and window I could see his face had turned a queasy shade, and I motioned that he move out of my way. Inspector Dew tried the door.

"Why, it's locked!"

Reaching through the broken pane, I stretched out my arm and, feeling about blindly, undid the mystery a moment later. The three of us then entered the room of the Ripper's latest victim, hearts pounding and each dealing with the appalling brutality of the attack in his own way.

A sickness rose in my throat, a reaction I had rarely before encountered on any case in my lengthy career. The room itself was hot enough to suffocate, and I clawed at the edges of my collar. I recalled that Jack's latest had been cheekily post-marked as "From Hell." The inscription was fitting.

Inspector Beck was back out the door and into the cold rain before anyone could catch him. I hadn't the heart to haul him back in. His presence in the small, stifling room was unnecessary. Inspector Dew seemed to harbour similar thoughts and stayed in the doorway, keeping an eye on both his fellow officer and the murmuring crowd that, magically enough, stayed somewhat distant.

The source of the immense heat in the room was that of the fireplace wherein raged an inferno of a blaze. By its light the rest of the home was shown. I eyed the broken window from this other side seeing, through my strong lens, evidence that I was not the first to enter or exit the room via the method I had demonstrated. I grumbled: what use was a locked door that anyone could reach in and open?

I turned and noted the spatters of blood upon the wall, the general disarray of the place, the abject poverty. I winced and moved forward to inspect the body—what was left of it. Unlike her predecessors, this woman had been stripped naked. She lay in the middle of the bed, her body turned towards the left side. Her legs had been spread wide, and her entire abdomen had been opened and rummaged for parts. Said organs had been systematically arrayed upon the nearby table. Or at least I guessed that they were there, kidneys and all. I would leave such gruesome tallying for the post mortem doctor to perform. Added to the sickening collection were her breasts and other bits of skin which had been carefully removed from the body. The face and arms sported their own mutilations, and as usual, the neck had been sliced open. In this case, the jagged wound touched bone. Jack's savagery had reached new depths.

Turning away and leaning against the window frame, I sought the cold air of the outside world. I looked and found my fingers trembled. Relief mingled with my horror. No man that I knew could do such a thing as this. The attack on this woman— they were the actions of a monster.

A methodical monster. I turned around and stared into the hot flames which licked at the edges of the hearth. I could see nothing obvious burning amongst the dancing blaze, and until it was brought under greater control, there was little I could do to delve into its contents.

I looked to Inspector Dew, giving my request, "If you might persuade Beck to fetch some water, I would be most appreciative."

THE DEVIL'S FIRE

CHAPTER 20

I could have been asking that the man produce a chicken from his waterproof with as strangely as he looked at me. He did not budge. I sighed. "For the fire, man. Let us see what our suspect has been burning here most industriously."

I retreated to the doorway and waited for the men to return. Within moments, two buckets of water had been brought. Carefully, I doused the flames, adding but a little water at a time so as not to wholly crush anything the killer might have sought to incinerate. Soon the small home was choked with a stinking cloud of steam. We escaped to the outside to catch our breaths and wait out the worst of it.

The first back through the door, I knelt in the wet ash of the dampened fire and set my lantern near upon the still-glowing hearth. Behind me, one of the detectives lit a lamp. I grunted my appreciation and reached for the poker to rake through the fire's leavings. Only barely dampened, the coals were so hot as to draw beads of sweat to my face and neck. The hairs on the back of my hands stung and shrivelled from the heat pouring off the hot masonry. Still I searched.

The room seemed to disappear behind my back. Intent on my game, me against the devil's fire, I picked at scraps and cinders. Embers rose up to snatch at my cuffs and char my knuckles. But I was committed. Here we had a link to our killer. Here was—at long last—something he most certainly did not wish us to find. And so find it I must.

My little pile of remains was growing. A chipped plate held my collection safe while I sifted and dug, added more air-stealing water to the hot slag, and dug some more. My eyes fairly streamed by the time I had found enough to return me to the table and to greater light.

Peering at the mess through my lens—the blasted thing kept fogging up on me—I saw snatches of writing. Pen and not print, a man's hand. The papers the Ripper had tried to burn had not become a total loss. Triumph led me to a short laugh which became a choking cough. I covered my face and continued my eager search.

"Ah!" The exclamation wheezed from me. Turning the small object 'round with the end of a utensil—companion to the plate I had borrowed—I puzzled over what I had found. Thin and longish but smaller than my finger, the little glass object had once been cylindrical, if its original shape were at all consistent. It had broken either through care- lessness or from the heat of the fire. The tiny label it had once borne had burnt itself into unrecognition.

I repeated my sifting and then returned to the still sweltering hearth. Two more tiny bottles unearthed themselves from amongst the sodden ash.

Though both had broken open, one was complete enough that I could yet read its label, in part.

Carrying the item to the light with the aid of a tarnished spoon, I peered close through my lens and read the fragmented words. "Made in accordance —" "—Cream" "London (Eng.)" "Poison"

I again hurriedly covered my mouth and read the last of the unobscured portion on the label: "Mercuria—"

I practically dropped the fragile treasure in my hurry to distance myself from it.

"Out. Everyone out," I gasped. The two Yard officials obeyed without question. The three of us tumbled back into the yard, myself motioning that we gain more distance.

"What is it?" Dew had gripped my arm.

"Mercury. The Ripper was burning some sort of prescriptive aid made from mercury." I gulped the clean night air and turned my face to the gently falling rain. "Fool that he is, the fire vaporized the medicine and made the air poisonous to breathe. Had I known, I wouldn't have doused the fire as I had."

"The villain."

"I doubt he considered his actions in that light." I shook my head, still drawing air as steadily as I could. "I expect he merely wished to rid himself of a thing that has weighed upon his heart. Something that, perhaps, he could not dispose of within his own dwelling place. So much of what he did in there changed from his previous killings—"

I paused and let my hammering pulse quiet itself. "He was brutal in the past, certainly. He again rendered his victim helpless before slitting her throat and doing the rest of his . . . ripping. But the passion was greater tonight. And he killed indoors rather than out. His vendetta has become decidedly personal, whether it's through having not killed in over a month's time or from some other unknown provocation. What he had done in the open, he has now done behind closed doors—and more so."

"With a fire like that, it's a wonder nobody noticed and came running."

"Come, I must re-examine the evidence. We have him, gentlemen. We have him at last." I covered my face and returned through the opened door of the gently steaming home.

I brought my plateful of debris to the lamplight and again picked through it as carefully as I could. Under my gentle touch, the ashen paper fell to dust. But I had found what I needed. I knew that writing. I knew the writer. I had spent the better part of my day reading his words.

"Hullo now, who's gone in?"

A familiar voice rang out in the night, and I straightened.

"In here, Inspector," I called.

Lestrade slunk into the room, eyeing me with an odd sort of restraint. I challenged him with a look, but he did not dare his question. Instead he said, "What do we know, Mr. Holmes?"

"Other than the fact that Jack appears to be a bit of an admirer of mine, has risen to new heights with his depravity, and is suffering from syphilis, not much." I moved to the side so that he might have a better view of the butchered body.

The stricken look which crossed his face brought a quaver of regret to my chest, and I rushed to ensure that the man did not fall from the shock of it all. "She would have bled out within seconds,

Lestrade. He killed her like the others, and she would not have had time or knowledge of the need to cry out. His further creativity came after."

"For the rest of us to suffer," he spat, moving forward. "What a cad. What a fiend." Sniffing, he looked around, "Why does the air stink and sweat as it does?"

Inspector Dew moved forward to offer his explanations. "Fire, sir. Blazing near out of control when we arrived. You can see where it burnt the spout off the tea kettle that stood nearby."

Lestrade peered close and gave a low whistle. "Likely burning evidence."

"Agreed," I stepped in once more. "And here is the best of the slim pickings. I leave it to you and your men, Lestrade, with my compliments. I would recommend, however, extreme caution with the little broken glass bottles. They, at one time, would have contained a cream which, when burned, produces the most undesirable of effects in the atmosphere. You'll find two such containers within the leavings on that plate—one has a better label than the other. Goodbye, Lestrade. And good luck."

I am certain he stared open-mouthed at my retreating form. I did not turn around to confirm this, however, and proceeded out into the lane where I hailed a carriage home. In another life, Watson would have whimsically accused me of lapsing into guesswork. I suppose he would have been right. But then, Lestrade had never strode far from the path of easy prediction.

The next day dawned cold and wet. The rain had continued through the night, in turns lashing the windows of 221b and pattering softly upon the panes. I had spent the night on the floor of the sitting room, my books spread about me and a map at my elbow. An urgent telegram had been sent to the Watson residence and another to the empty house on 37 Mary Street. I had little hope that either would find their intended recipient. Each of my own watchers upon the houses had not reported a sighting of the doctor. I no longer had any expectation for his return.

But I had made good use of my time. My hasty research session yielded up a short list of chemists in the East End. With luck, one might be persuaded to give up a five foot seven syphilitic man with a moustache who had needed mercury cream. With great luck, that name might be on the list of men whom I still suspected of having absconded with Watson's manuscripts during the doctor's aim for publication. Manuscripts that had, sadly, met their fiery end in a slum in Spitalfields.

Adjusting my disguise over the breakfast table, for this time I certainly could not go as myself, I reinvigorated both body and soul. I had work. I had direction. Hope? That would come when it may. Speaking directly to that flavour of emotion, I sent off another set of telegrams and checked in with Billy, who had come 'round to loaf at my front door. I told him briefly of my aims should . . . well, should anyone of importance come calling. And with that I stepped fully out into a rain-soaked London and, turning my collar up against the chilly air, made for the Underground. A short ride later, I resurfaced in another part of town and found the first of nine chemists' shops on my list.

The first proved fruitless. No amount of pleading nor threatening would have them giving up the treatment that my character wanted for his condition.

Raising my trouser leg to demonstrate the tell-tale rash only made matters worse. "We're not that kind of shop. Try the one down the lane," and a thinly veiled insinuation that the police might be interested in my activities, sent me on my dejected way.

A repeat performance at the next produced slightly better results. They, however, used an entirely different ointment which rendered the place useless for my purposes. My purchase, forced on me by a rather sweet yet indomitable portly man behind the counter, came with a rather stern lecture on the topic of morality and proper conduct. I promised I would reform my ways and made my exit.

The third through sixth locales produced more of the same. But it was the seventh shop which gave me my answer at long last. Hid amongst a huddle of dilapidated buildings, I could not help but feel a shudder of apprehension as I approached its door. The whole place had an air of neglect and disrepute about it. However could a person trust what physics this place dispensed?

I entered and found myself facing as seedy an individual as had ever graced the medicine-adjacent world. The man smiled, somehow managing to inject an oily sensation into the expression. His words came out equally slick.

Dutifully I began my complaint, rolling up a pant-leg so as to reveal the false rash I had painstakingly painted on just that morning. Tut-tutting over my predicament, he rummaged about and returned with a small glass phial. While not a man readily given to outbursts of passion, it took great effort on my part to not simply leap about the room in triumph. Instead I tried, "Naw. This'n 'ere 's been

175

somat a friend o' mines been usin'. Said it gives 'im the quakes."

"I am sorry, my man. But you must be mistaken. I've not had anyone using this and giving complaint. Your friend must have got his cure elsewhere or some long time ago."

"Naw, 'e says you 'spific'ly. Jack. 'S name is Jack."

The chemist's mask slipped for an instant. He shook his head. "Well now, I can't go around naming names, either. Just as you want discretion from me, I provide it for all who patronize this shop."

I straightened and, dropping my accent, placed a scorched and mostly complete glass phial upon the counter next to the first. "Then you are protecting a man who has murdered some half a dozen women and aims higher still. I will find him with or without your aid, but it is your word here and now that may save the next victim from this butcher."

Startled, the man began to sputter, "You're a—"

"Private consulting detective and therefore you are not speaking with a police official. Your discretion to those who deserve it remains intact. Jack the Ripper, however . . ." I let the name hang in the air.

"I know the man. But don't you tell nobody else that I tol' you," he caved at long last and leaned forward to whisper both a name and address.

I recoiled, and my breath and blood seized. My mind blanked. Surely I had misheard.

He saw the disbelief on my face and grinned. " 'S not what you'd call a cozy cottage, but 'e lives there, you can be sure o' that."

"Jack."

"You can call 'im Jack all you want. You and them papers. But 'e goes by 'J.' 'round these parts."

"Watson."

176

"Tha's what I said. It's what 'e goes by: J. Watson. Some sorta writer chap, I think. Wouldn't have pegged 'im for murder though."

I wanted to disbelieve him. Frankly, I wanted to leap over the counter and force a different answer from his lips. I did neither. Instead I stood within the shabby shop, so utterly deflated, utterly crushed, that for the first time in my life I wished the earth would simply open up and swallow me whole.

"You a'right?"

With a brittle smile, I thanked him for his time, reassumed my disguise and reached to take back my bottle from the counter. It disappeared into my greasy palm, leaving behind a handsome coin in its place. The chemist's eyes bulged as he looked from coinage to me and back again. He looked as though he was seeing Father Christmas in the flesh, and I almost laughed. He said, "Thank 'e, sir. Both for—"

I left before he could further embarrass himself with his misplaced gratitude.

Disappearing around the next corner, I took out a pen and quickly jotted the address upon my shirt cuff. The chemist was right. It did not ring in my memory as a residential quarter. But I had an address. And so I must follow it.

The clouds had partnered with the wind to rain further misery down upon London. Dusk was coming on swiftly on this overcast, late autumn day. Left with little alternative considering my destination and the limits of the Underground, I hailed a cab and rode south and east towards the river.

While I rode, I fingered the revolver in my pocket and considered my position. I still did not believe my oily informant. He believed himself, that much was certain. But—I could not. And would never. Not until Watson's face stared out at me from the shadowy personage of Jack the Ripper. Not until I had him in custody and had his confession stated aloud.

Not until I had no other choice.

But where was Watson in all of this, if not here? What was his secret if not this very track that I pursued?

I shut my mind to Dr. John Watson, my friend, and focused on what I knew of Jack, the Whitechapel Horror.

There hope slithered in. It was a game against me. It must be! Had Jack, again, been one step ahead? Had he put his evidence into the fire knowing exactly in what manner I would track him? The man I pursued was undoubtedly dangerous. And I had been forced to work alone through circumstance and my own fear and pride. My loyalty. With a pang, I considered how I might have tried to trust Lestrade in the end by sending him word of my activities instead of, as he had rightfully accused me, keeping all for myself. In any event, the only life I had directly endangered this night was my own. Well, my own and that of one J. Watson, alias Jack the Ripper.

DEATH IN THE EAST END

CHAPTER 21

The fitful wind and rain had risen to a soaking gale by the time I reached the hodgepodge district of the London Docks. Water sluiced down from the tall buildings that surrounded the narrow lane upon which I stood. The weather had hastened twilight on its way the same as it had chased most folk into homes and clubs, pubs, and anywhere else where a warming fire could be had. In spite of the gathering gloom, I chose my pistol over my lantern and proceeded towards where my game sat within his den.

A series of squalid buildings lined the street whose address I had been given. I picked out the number with some difficulty and, again, felt a pang that I had chosen to eschew assistance from Lestrade or anyone else. I considered the police station that huddled amongst its quiet industry-minded neighbours not five blocks off. But I was certain that a sodden wild-eyed man breaking in their doorway with tales of Jack the Ripper was sure to go poorly. I moved on from the thought.

I was forced to use my lockpicks on the door to the Ripper's lair, hissing in alarm when the lock clicked none-too-quietly under my ministrations. Granted, with the rain still pouring down and growing rumbles of thunder in the distance, my observation and subsequent tension might have been mere nerves. I entered the dark and dirty hallway beyond, wishing I might use my light after all. I stopped. I listened. All was quiet save for the dull roar of the worsening storm outside. The wind whistled through ill-fitted windows, pried at loose shutters and boards, yet no human sound met my ears. I moved onwards, trying each of the rickety stair treads with but part of my weight before trusting to them not to betray my presence.

The first storey showed signs of life. Even less hospitable than the encampment within Watson's Mary Street house, the spare furniture spoke of desperation and despair. By the light of a lone candle still burning on an overturned basket that seemed to serve as both nightstand and dining table, I could see clothing had been strewn about on chairs and the like. Surprised, I noted several fine pieces amongst his strange collection of haberdashery. Our Jack could go to the theatre or work on the docks and blend in well in both instances—were I not around, of course, to point out the finer points of posture, bone structure of the hands, and other minutiae.

Readying my revolver and turning so that I faced the door, I moved to inspect the candle. The drippings told me that the occupant had not left the room very long ago. Several empty bottles upon the ground gave me a good estimation of his errand.

Drawing a sharp breath, I steeled myself for the

search. Would Jack have left his bloodied knife in his sanctuary? Might I make discovery of it before his return? An unsteady step in the hall told me that, no, I would not have this opportunity. Exposed in the barren room and forced to make a hasty decision, I snuffed the candle and dove for the darkest corner near the door.

This was my first error of judgment.

Jack knew his building's many eccentricities. He was familiar with which steps creaked and could betray his approach. He, too, knew wherein to place his light so as to keep it safe from drafts. Through the jamb, I saw a dark form of a man tense in the hallway, hesitate, and then run.

I gave chase.

The two of us clattered down the stairs, he far ahead and myself hardly gaining. For we traversed ground upon which he was expert, just as he had learned the particulars of the district wherein he had hunted. A mad scramble over a fence left my lungs heaving and my steps lagging. Intent on the shadowy figure whom I pursued, I pushed myself to greater speed, glancing off rough brickwork as my prey chose narrow and twisted pathways in an attempt to lose me.

Another fence, another set of narrow and crooked stairs and I half-feared I had lost him. Until a bolt from the heavens illuminated all. Jack's silhouette shown plainly for one instant, and then all was blackness once more. I fumbled for my pocket lantern, still running.

No steadiness of nerve could coax a light from the infernal device. The wild elements snatched at my feeble flame and doused the lamp before it could take. Forced to abandon my efforts, I thrust the untrustworthy device back into my pocket and trusted to street lighting and lightning to aid my eyes. The man was yet in my sights, and his steps were growing laboured, his small limp more pronounced as we leapt over and past the obstacles that fell within our zig-zag path. I readied my pistol but found no target.

I would not shoot an unarmed man. I needed him alive, and I needed his confession.

Our overall trajectory led us southward, and I indulged in a grim smile. If he made for anywhere save Wapping Station, I had him. Jack's steps were tiring. I saw the man slip more than once during our harried chase. The limp had deepened.

And then he disappeared.

Slipping out from a passage betwixt two filthy and close-pressed buildings and into High Street, I found I confronted an empty road. I swivelled my gaze up to the dark buildings on either side of the street. Left or right? For Jack to take the left was to repeat the chase he had only narrowly won. Too, he loved to play my game. The more complex option would be the most tantalizing to his nature. Therefore, the hulking, multi-storey wharves held the most promise.

Sidling close to the nearest building, I saw an ill-shut door. Closer still and I could see it had been broken in. Rain spatter within confirmed for me that I had regained the scent. Kneeling, I tried again to coax my lantern to life. This time it obeyed.

Swinging the illumination out in front of me, I could see the Ripper's path marked out in shining droplets of water. Our chase resumed, taking me up stairs and through wide halls. We weaved through great stacks of barrels and around offices. The bright trail of rainwater was lessening with each ascension to the next storey but, by now, I needed little of that to tell where I might find my man. I could hear his heavy breathing in the darkness. His steps echoed in the cavernous rooms through which the Ripper fled. Catching sight of him again in the next flash of light from the raging storm outside, I abandoned my lantern in favour of my gun. Another flight of steps disappeared beneath our frenzied feet.

And then: an empty room. I crested the topmost stair and found myself alone in the long, slope-roofed space that topped the dockside building. Motion at the far end drew my eye, and I ran forward, seeing legs disappearing up through an open hatch. There I paused, aiming my revolver upward and gauging whether or not Jack was intent on mere escape or a solution more deadly. Trusting to luck, I shimmied up onto the roof of the wharf and looked about for my man.

He had gained some distance during my hesitation, but in the wide space I had an easy target. I aimed. I paused.

I pursued.

"Stop!" I cried. But the storm drowned out my plea.

We scrambled along the pitched roof, slipping and sliding as we went. The chase grew ever more desperate. And then, the next slope proved too much for the Ripper. Trying his footing, he made it but halfway to the crest and then skidded back down to the long flat alley in which we both stood not sixty paces apart. I could see that his lungs pained him, and he stumbled as he backed away. I fared little better.

The next flash of lighting showed me the knife in

his hand. I could see him tense. I, too, tensed, readying my aim. Turning, he looked downward behind him. His placement was such that he stood between my mercy and certain death in the river far below.

The rain had become pelting ice, and the wind howled, screaming between us. Neither moved, neither flinched as he completed his contemplation of the options left him. Without turning, he shifted, his free hand seeming to slide towards the pocket of his long coat, though without clear light I could not be certain of it. I moved ever closer. Fifty paces now separated us. That and the storm's unrelenting fury. Head still down and away, Jack let his knife drop from his hand.

He now turned to gaze at me, but in the dark I could not see his face. "Holmes!"

My heart all but stopped.

The voice was unmistakable, even muted as it was by sleet and gale. Watson.

I inched forward, stopping as Jack the Ripper levelled at me the object he had pulled from his pocket. A revolver. Service issue? My own weapon trained upon the Whitechapel Fiend, I tensed, but I could not shoot. Not yet.

I needed to see his face.

My hesitation was broken by a flash and the deafening report of the Ripper's gun. I ducked, too late, and felt the sting of his bullet in my arm. I watched, dumbfounded, as he spun sideways and down . . . caught by a shot that had come from behind me. My brain hurried to catch up, confirming that, yes, the crack of the pistol had been too loud, too ill-timed with the flash to have been from his revolver alone.

I turned to find another man on the roof not twenty steps behind. He was running towards me, and my eyes widened in disbelief. Watson!

Shouting, Watson gestured wildly at me, and I turned back to gaze upon where the Ripper had slumped down onto the roof. We both ran to catch our man. But before either Watson or I could get there, Jack rose to his feet and, turning, made a leap off the building's lip.

We raced to the edge to find nothing save for a knife, some small drops of blood, and a battered old hat the wind itself took away an instant later. It tumbled through the air and down into the foaming Thames which waited below.

It was over then.

There we stood for some time, side by side at death's edge, until Watson, sensible man of medicine, remarked, "You're hurt."

I had not realized I had clapped my hand over the point on my coat sleeve where the Ripper's bullet had left its mark. I nodded in assent of the doctor's diagnosis, and we turned to pick our way back to the hatch that had led us up onto the roof.

Between there and Baker Street, the only words from either of us came from Watson. And they consisted of his hailing and directing the cab in which we rode. Arriving at 221, he produced his key and, giving me a sheepish smile, let us in. By then my steps lagged so that I allowed him to assist me up the stairs and into our apartment, even sitting still long enough for him to inspect and dress the shallow wound that graced the upper portion of my right arm.

We then sat, I with an undiluted whisky and my cherrywood pipe, he with brandy and cigarette. At length, he ventured, "You recall, Holmes, the incident surrounding my pocket-watch at the outset of my wife's case last year?"

"I do." I flicked hooded eyes his way.

He barrelled onward, heedless of my silent warning. "And I claimed both astonishment and awe over your ability to infer so much about its previous owner when I gave it over to you for analysis."

"I recall you being quite angry with me. You accused me of having looked into your private affairs rather than applying pure deductive reasoning."

He smiled at my mild correction. "Yes. Well, Holmes, in any event you were wrong on one particular. And such a fact I was eager to conceal from you. It was on that day that the lie began, the one which I have lived these many long months."

I sighed and put aside my pipe. Steepling my fingers, I sat back in my chair and regarded my friend. "Your brother. He is not dead."

"No, Holmes, he is not." At this admission, Watson's face carried within it such anguish that, for a moment, I feared he would not continue. But he mastered himself, saying, "I would not wish death upon my own brother. In some ways, however, your erroneous interment of him might have been the gentler fate."

Watson rose and moved to stand before the fire. There he paused, hands on the mantle and his face towards the flames, as though stuck in a grave fit of indecision. "What I have next to say to you, Holmes, will be terribly unpleasant. I had hoped to keep you from it. For my honour and for your own sake.

"But pressed as I am and with the words that have passed between us . . . Well, you are owed the truth, painful as it may be." He took from the corner of the mantle my morocco case containing my hypodermic syringe, and I felt my breath go dead within me. Turning, he read the look in my eyes, saw my dread for what it was. He had been kind enough to leave the bottle where it lay.

"My unfortunate brother, Sherlock, has been in the grips of a persistent morphine addiction for nigh on fifteen years."

"And he lives in a three-storey home on the south side of Mary Street between Alfred and Harley Streets."

"Yes." With that bleak acknowledgment, Watson returned to his chair, though he retained the little wooden case. There he sat, unspeaking until, with a steadying breath, he began, "I suppose that I give too much credit to my brother if I lay upon him the charge of having inspired my choice of profession. At the time of my taking my degree I was only obliquely aware of the terrible inclination that lay within my brother's makeup. The behaviours that so distressed our parents? I thought to be weakness of character, of morality, and so strove to be a shining example—light to his dark. I aspired to be an army doctor. This so as to make something of myself and to excise any potential shortcomings within my own character under the constraints of military discipline. All while hopefully making a difference within the world.

"And at times over the years, my influence had seemed to set my brother aright. But then he would fall to old habits amongst old friends, surrender to old cravings. He had not the need for your excitations of brain, you understand, but always felt as though he needed something in his life, the very thing morphine promised him.

"That empty promise." Watson's voice grew gravelled with feeling. "It worsened when Hamish inherited and found himself with some means. The Afghan campaign was the hardest. While there I had no control or knowledge over what he did and could only pray that Providence continue to watch over him as it always had done. And when at last I came home, I did so with a greater understanding of the world and its intricacies and fearing the worst for my brother. My own health had been devastated, shattered by a Jezail bullet. Strangely enough, my weakness proved his strength. In having to see to my needs, he forgot his own for a time.

"And then the curse returned with a fearful roaring, and I found that I could not stay."

The emotion which had clouded Watson's horizon now overtook him. "I . . . I abandoned him, Holmes! For I could not, in my weakened state, do what needed doing."

I waited, impassive lest I add to my friend's display. The storm lessened, and his shoulders ceased to quake from their attempts at holding in his agony of thought. The dark flood of memories had come and had gone.

I ventured, "And so you were led here, to me, to Baker Street—"

"And renewed purpose, yes." It was with a fervent glint in his eye that Watson's gaze met mine. "I recovered. I thrived. To my surprise, so did Hamish. It would seem my condition and the choices it forced me to make had brought his own life into greater focus. Thus went the pattern of highs and lows. Luxury and poverty in turns. All whilst I turned a blind eye and rebuilt my life here in London and away from his unquiet demons.

"He did drink, Holmes. That, too, was a correct observation on your part. In time he came to enjoy every vice save, I believe, for opium, though with his capacity for secrecy and utter deception I cannot be sure. He followed me here, moving to London, to the Mary Street house, two summers back. I had only just managed to reconnect with him—saving our father's watch from the pawnbrokers and electing to treat this recalcitrant patient myself—when Miss Morstan's case fell upon our doorstep. My impertinent test of your powers on my father's timepiece was meant to be my opening. I needed to broach the subject with you of my unfortunate brother."

"But then you had not expected I should hit so near the truth with my deductions."

"I had not expected that, within that very hour, I should so thoroughly fall under Miss Morstan's spell!" Watson shook his head and sat back in his chair. "The case then occupied all of our energies until it became too late for me to continue the aborted discussion. You'll recall that you were only mildly congratulatory on my pending nuptials. I feared— I thanked my lucky stars I had not been allowed to confess that terrible truth. Under the greater time and distance afforded by my moving out and buying a practice, I was able to better consider what that truth might do to our friendship.

"What if you thought that I saw you as a project, a patient and nothing more? What if . . . what if you chose to cut me from your life as I had my own brother? I could not face it. And Mary? She had no need for such baseness to touch her new life with me. As you had proclaimed it, my brother was dead."

"Yet being a medical man, and a good brother, you continued to help him as best you could."

"How could I not, Holmes! The guilt gnawed at me. Without his aid to me after my return to England, I might have ended up ailing away to nothing. I owed him. I owed him my life, and I owed him my absolute discretion. As I, too, owed you and Mary for the reasons I have told."

I eyed the case in his hand understanding, in part, why he believed he could not have told me. I had other objections, however. "But your wife! Of all the loving, caring creatures on the planet . . . !"

"It was an injurious, wounding, poisonous truth, Holmes. And what I dared not tell you, I could not confess to her."

Of all the blows. This, this is what staggered me most in John's confession. The unerring trust and regard at the heart of his great deception. That he would value my favour so dearly, that he could concern himself with my susceptibilities so much so that he would rather live a horrid lie than burden his friend's conscience; it humbled me, and I found myself with nothing to say. My heart was too full for words.

He, too, did not speak for long moments after. Instead he sat and waited, putting aside the offending box which contained my worst vice and weakness, a personal failing which had plagued Watson all this time and had been mirrored in the suffering of his brother.

At length I ventured, "But why continue the lie? When your own life was falling apart around you?"

"Because I had not considered how my protection of Hamish's situation put me under the suspicions that you levelled upon me. Not until I felt it too late to make my excuses. Honestly, Holmes, how could you?"

"My dear Watson, you saw, firsthand, what we have been up against; you know my methods. As it was, I said nothing to Lestrade, seeking even to conceal the facts most problematic to your continued safety as long as I dared."

"But, Holmes—!"

I allowed him his anger. He had earned it.

Flinching, I waited for a condemnation which never fell. John instead settled forward in his chair, attentive student—nay, partner—once more.

I leaned forward and spoke. "Consider the following. Your actions over the past six months have been decidedly odd. A terribly bloody case comes up in the East End, and my sensitive and caring friend asks that I not involve myself in its investigation. Lestrade brings me on in such a way that I cannot easily refuse, and suddenly my friend Watson is back in his old chair at Baker Street, asking questions."

"I worried about your constitution. I knew how the macabre draws you, Holmes. But this seemed beyond the pale and holding none of the usual earmarks of a case that best engages your talents."

"Murk of a different sort, yes. Consider then, my suspicions, already roused due to—as you say—the state of my nerves. I find two cigarette stubs at the first scene I visit. They are stamped with the mark of your tobacconist. Over that I find a scrawled message. Not unusual within the annals of crime, true, but indicating further the level of sophistication our man had. Add to that the physical description of our suspect borne by the state of the crime scene and various eyewitness testimonies." I enumerated each point upon my open palm with a jab of my finger.

"I don't have to listen to this." Truly angered now, Watson rose to his feet.

"And then there's the telegram you did not send to yourself. The one that would have read 'Urgent —' " I smiled. He sat, stunned. "The message would then have arrived here to find its way into my curious and meddlesome fingers. Correspondence for you here? At this address? You knew I could not resist such a morsel."

"How did you—?"

"I followed you. As I said, my suspicions had been roused. You, in fact, greeted me on the stoop of the office after having changed your mind about sending such an obvious misdirect to my very doorstep."

"It was you!" Flabbergasted, he could only shake his head in awe.

My smile became a knowing smirk. I could not help it. Watson was forever complimentary to my self-confidence. I continued, "From there I had confirmation of a second mystery in my hands. Whatever was Dr. John Watson up to? But Lestrade's case kept nosing in. By now I had the Ripper's first letter in my hand."

"And the comment about the ears . . ."

"Plus several other small points, yes. Things were not looking well for you. If I could only keep Lestrade from the scent long enough to clear things up. As you said yourself, how could I think such a thing of you? My case was incomplete. I knew my Dr. Watson. And yet . . . for my Boswell to pointedly deny any recollection of one of our more memorable cases? I set Wiggins on your trail. Am I correct in my surmise that it was your own 'irregular' who caught Billy in his act of surveillance?"

"That which was condemning me in your eyes was serving me, yes. I used your methods against you. Having recognized your little street force about, I engaged some of my own. I felt I needed to protect my secret."

"Ha! Well done, Watson. Were they, incidentally, occupied in informing you of my whereabouts this evening?"

"And the other night, yes. They proved instrumental in my managing to spirit Hamish out of the house before the Yard set its watch upon the place."

"The eyes and ears of London, those boys. Up until your near arrest at the entrance to Mitre Square, I thought I was ahead of your problem though I had remained ever-lagging on the Ripper business. That morning, however, the coincidence was proving too great for even me to overlook. After we parted ways at the police station, you said you were returning home. That you did not but, instead, rode further into the East End was reported to me by Perth."

I trailed off, needing to brace myself for my next conclusions of fact. That the very profession which had brought us together could well drive us apart . . . ? I was sorely tempted to leave the rest to Watson's vivid imagination. Of course, I did not. "I discovered that Jack the Ripper's first letter was written while the paper lay atop a copy of *Beeton's Christmas Annual*. Page 49 of *A Study in Scarlet*. From that, in a move of desperate hope, I visited Mary. There, in your sitting room, I heard for the first time the astonishing news that my friend John Watson had been staying with me on over half a dozen occasions within the past few months. The clothes hid within your satchel in the corner of your study—"

"Oh!" Watson groaned. "I had forgotten about those. Hamish, in one of his withdrawal-induced fits of rage, threw a table lamp at the wall behind me. It shattered, leaving its oil on my coat. I tried to wash it off in a basin but gave it up as hopeless."

"Paraffin, my dear Doctor, has proven quite serviceable as a remover of blood stains. Though it does tend to leave behind its distinctive tell-tale odour. I would consider the coat a loss, incidentally. My nose, upon opening the bag, detected the bloom of mould."

"What else?" Watson was resigned to his fate at last.

"Besides my having already covered up my noticing the crimson stain upon your shirt sleeve back at the Commercial Street Station on the morning of September 30th? Your memorandum-book within your desk confirmed the poorest of alibis for every night in question."

"Nights I had elected to stay with Hamish."

"On Mary Street, yes. The cryptic notes on each of those dates, I'll admit, struck no small chill in my heart, Watson. I was careful not to tell Mary of the extent of my discoveries and left her with explicit instructions not to let on what she knew of the lie you told each of us. She was to contact me the instant it was next repeated. With your future appointments with mysterious 'Mary' now in hand, I had my suspicions of when to next be ready."

"But I did come calling on you. You were not home."

"You can imagine that foolish vigil, yes. Me at your house while you waited at mine for my return. The next occasion, on October 14th, proved more fruitful."

Neither of us wished to rehash the heated discussion had outside the elder Watson's house from three weeks prior. That wound, like the rest, needed more time to heal.

Watson, dear Watson, spoke first into the long silence. "When you lay it all out that way, I'm half convinced of it myself, Holmes. However did you keep the police—keep yourself—from clapping me in irons, just as a precaution?"

"The thought crossed my mind, yes. But that was a move from which there was no backing down," I commented drily. "You'll remember that I was working against Lestrade once he had set his sights upon you and, in the end, with the real killer at the other end of my revolver, that I did not shoot."

It was my turn to demand more silence. He waited for me to gather my thoughts. At length, my reliving of the horrid moment cleared itself from my brain. "With the rain blinding me as it did, I could not be certain of my man. I knew it my killer. I knew it by his gun, by the facts that had led me to his den at last—the breadcrumb trail of your paperwork, much of which, by the way, has met an unfortunate end in a Whitechapel hovel. You might want to have a word with your publisher on how they secure their documents. I knew Jack the Ripper by the manner in which he fled. But I did not know if it were you. And so I hesitated."

"That hesitation almost proved costly, Holmes." It was all the chiding I would receive from him.

I nodded, not quite trusting my voice to the thanks which lived in my heart. I substituted, "Go home, Watson. Go home to your wife. Tell Mary all of your part in this. She is a loving, forgiving woman. She will understand."

Watson met my gaze. Relieved hope lived in those eyes.

Giving him a tired smile and rising to my feet, I bade him farewell and promised him that I was, myself, leaving so that I might give word to Lestrade of the case's closure. If Watson took the more circuitous route home, the police presence in James Street would be withdrawn by the time he arrived.

And with that imperfect goodbye, Watson walked out of 221B Baker Street.

I was not to see him again until the end of the year.

EULOGY

CHAPTER 22

The *Aberdeen Journal*, in its Tuesday, December 25, 1888 edition, reported that:

Christmas Eve, so far as London is concerned, presented the worst features of an inclement winter's night. The holidays began on Saturday, scarcely a single shop of a representative class being open. The morning of Christmas Eve began in dull, warm weather, and as twilight came down upon the dreary and depressed multitudes heavy rain added its influence to the prevalent gloom. "A green Yule maketh a fat kirkyard." So runs the legend, and certainly there is not much health in the elements amid which we live this Christmas. In Whitechapel an eerie feeling took hold of the inhabitants, owing to an impression or suspicion or fear that Christmas Day might dawn upon a new horror. The police have naturally relaxed their vigilance, and, in an official sense, the crimes of the autumn have been well-nigh forgotten.

The poor inhabitants of this benighted region, however, hold "Jack the Ripper" in a species of superstitious dread, believing that he chooses high holidays and fast-days for his murderous forays.

This paper, amongst many others, littered the floor of 221B Baker Street two days after its printing. It was correct in two particulars. The first being that the weather had been utterly depressing of late. The second being the lessening of the police presence in and around London's East End, but for very different reasons than the men of news had forwarded.

Inspector Lestrade and I had had many long talks over the past several weeks. Per my promise to Watson, I had gone to the Yard detective the very night of the Ripper's disappearance and made my extraordinary statement. Lestrade had listened to my tale with an alternating mix of surprise and frank mistrust upon his rat-like features. But in the end, he knew I would not lie about so important a thing.

As to the reasoning for the Ripper's actions, the intentions behind the gruesome slayings, and his knowledge of myself and Watson and the rest, without Jack's testimony we were forced into the realms of pure conjecture. Lestrade visited the dilapidated East End chemist who had given up our man and saw for himself how the charred bottles of mercury cream had provided us our lead in the end. There, too, we could begin to guess at motive. Syphilis closes many doors to a person, and through interviews, hearsay, and a bit of digging in military records, we began to piece together some bits of Jacky's history. Contracting—or at least displaying signs of—that terrible disease, the Ripper had run from his attachment, eventually landing in London's East End under an assumed name and holding dubious connexions.

The police and myself pored over the scene of the Ripper's hideout and found further small clues to shore up our case. His stationary supply, a bottle of his ever dramatic red ink, both became property of Scotland Yard. I discovered how he had tried his own hand at fictional accounts of cases that might have fit within the purview 221B Baker Street. These he had signed "J. Watson," though his prose was nowhere near as elevated as the work of our own dear doctor's.

It appeared that, in losing his own future, he had seized upon that of another. A very worn, heavily annotated copy of *Beeton's* '87 was found amongst the Ripper's things. In hearing this, the doctor attached to the Metropolitan Police forwarded his own opinion: monomania. By finding something within Watson's story that he himself lacked—what Jack believed himself cheated out of through the curse of his disease—he had chosen to insert himself in the narrative through any means necessary. Thus the Ripper styled himself as both antagonist and narrator to the story that he controlled.

Through our efforts, all suspicions upon Dr. Watson of James Street were lifted, the business of the East End Horror was laid aside, and life returned to something akin to normal. I resumed my work, disturbing my landlady with the usual parade of odd visitors and odder hours. And Scotland Yard rebuilt its uneasy peace with my methods, keeping me informed of the goings-on in London's criminal underbelly and requesting some small assistance from me when needed.

The body of Jack the Ripper we never recovered. His knife, I hear, was misplaced—a fitting end to the compendium of errors which had plagued the case.

All was calm; all was bright. But for the holidays, I sat in languid boredom surrounded by my cloud of newsprint and playing melancholy airs upon my Stradivarius. It was in this state that Watson found me on the evening of the 27th.

"And this is how the great Sherlock Holmes passes the ending of a year," he proclaimed. He stood in the doorway, beaming at me in a manner that told me all had been forgiven.

I rose to greet my friend. "Good to see you, Watson. Do sit down. Drink?"

"No, thank you, Holmes. I'm due back home to Mary and cannot stay long." He sat. "But I could not pass Baker Street without my feet turning themselves to the steps of 221 and my hand reaching for its door. How are you, old man?"

I waved off the question, the gesture its own answer. "And you, Watson? How are you and yours?"

A shadow crossed through his face before he gave answer. "Mary forgave me my ill behaviour. And Hamish—he succumbed two weeks ago. The house on Mary Street lies vacant save for his tortured spirit."

"I am sorry, Watson."

A pained smile flickered over his lips. "I thank you, Holmes."

His eyes then darted to the fireplace, an involuntary check on me that brought a flush of embarrassment to his cheeks. No, my morocco case with its hypodermic syringe had not moved since Watson's last replacing of it upon the mantle.

He rose and moved to the sideboard. "Whisky and water?"

"I thought you were not staying long." I flicked my eyes to him.

"It's Christmas, Holmes."

"That it is, Watson." I accepted the glass and raised it to my friend.

Together we sat in companionable silence, and between one tick of the clock and the next, in the crackle of the fire and the sound of late December snow slapping wetly against the window which over-looked Baker Street, I could feel that still-absent part of my life slide back into place. That missing piece, it fit somewhere near my heart, and I turned away so that Watson might not see the tear which dampened the corner of my eye.

"Jack the Ripper may be dead, but his actions are indelible," Watson broke into my thoughts, drawing my attention upon him. He gazed into the fire, his eyes seeing not Baker Street, I am sure, but something akin to a windblown rooftop on a cold November night.

"As are all our deeds, Watson. Good or ill."

Bleak despair looked at me from my friend's face as he turned to ask, "Then whatever am I to do, Holmes? It is my writings that inspired his actions. My word that drove his knife."

"His motives were his own. His exploits, too. Jack the Ripper sought fame, yes, but what he found was infamy. I've little doubt there will be more like him, whether or not you ever again put pen to paper."

"Surely not, Holmes!"

"For every action, a consequence, Watson."

"Then I am to blame."

"Now, now." I sat upright, annoyed he should so doggedly pursue that line. I fixed him a stern eye. "You haven't invented crime. One could hardly say that you even celebrate it. No. You stand clearly upon the shores of goodness and hope, my dear Watson. If anything, your tales shine as a warning against those who would dare do ill against the innocent. A beacon of love and homage to intellectual triumph. No, Doctor, do not blame yourself for the darker hearts of other men. Rather, I would ask that you cling to your position and shout it from every rooftop in London. And beyond. Which puts me in mind to an introduction I've been meaning to make."

Watson's questioning glance followed me as I rose and crossed the room. There I rifled through the corner bookshelf, speaking all the while, "After your little . . . experiment . . . at the holidays last year, I received a caller, a gentleman who was much interested in your work."

With a triumphant "ha!" I pulled out a bent copy of *Beeton's Christmas Annual* 1887.

Seeing the object in my hand, Watson beamed. "Holmes, I am touched. So many of those papers went into the dustbin with the ribbons and paper in January. I hadn't realized you saved a copy."

"I didn't. This is Mrs. Hudson's."

"Oh."

Flipping open the thin magazine, I took out a piece of paper and handed it off.

He read it with crestfallen eyes. "Newnes. *The Strand Magazine*? Really, Holmes, if this is your way of telling me in a roundabout way that I ought not publish these accounts—!"

"While at first I did not agree with your story-telling ambitions, I have come to believe your journaling may yet serve some greater good. After all, if the public is aware of our endeavours here at 221B Baker Street, it may give some criminals pause."

"Our endeavours, Holmes?"

"But of course, my dear Watson. I do need someone around to keep me somewhat levelheaded. And besides, I have absolutely no intent on putting any of these entertaining little intellectual problems into print myself. That is your gift, Doctor. Amongst many, many others."

With tears in his eyes, Watson gave his fervent thanks for the rare compliment.

It was then that I had to gently caution my friend, "I would ask, however, that you never recount the story of our involvement in the case of Jack the Ripper."

He stared at me. "But, Holmes, would people not notice the omission if I were to eventually publish all the rest? A gap of four months' time . . ."

"I grant you full artistic license in that respect, Watson. Make up a case to your own liking to fill the space. Something sensational. Supernatural. The sort of thing people don't think to look much past. Besides, your grasp for the intellectual essentials of a case is one thing, your attention to detail on dates, locations, and people may be less so."

"To protect the honour of your clients."

His innocent dismissal of my mild criticism brought a small smile to my lips, a twitch of a correction that I wisely aborted. We again settled in to smoke and drink and recount our latest adventures. I had just begun to describe to him the curious business of a recent jewel heist and the investigation upon which my services had been engaged by the Countess of Morcar when a sharp ring of the bell had both Watson and I sitting bolt upright. There was no mistaking the glimmer in his eyes, an excitement hastily hid away lest he put me out by it.

The seventeen steps up to our door thundered with the heavy tread of a working man and lighter step of our landlady. Watson and I both rose to our feet in anticipation. The door opened to reveal a man in the utmost state of excitement.

He paused, hat in hand—and hat on head, I noted, with some surprise—and looked from me to the doctor and back again.

"Mr. Holmes," he began, "I have just now had the most extraordinary shock of my life."

"Sit down, if you'll please. Dr. Watson, this is Mr. Peterson, who found a lost goose in the road not two days ago." I gestured to an open seat. "Sit and proceed to tell us about he whose hat has so shaken your nerves, for clearly your own is still upon your head."

"That's just it, Mr. Holmes. I do not know the man. He dropped the hat in Goodge Street two days back. That along with that Christmas goose I had come 'round to ask you about. I made my own little inquiries but, after two days, we were forced to eat the goose lest it spoil." He gulped, eyes bulging. Watson moved closer, ready with brandy should it be needed. "My wife, sir. She found this in the crop."

Quaking, our visitor opened his palm and thrust its contents at me.

A massive blue jewel winked in the firelight.

"The Countess of Morcar's missing diamond," Watson ejaculated.

"Indeed." I accepted the jewel and held it to the light. "Thank you, Peterson, I know your conscience had been much burdened by the thought of a poor family going without its Christmas feast. This, I presume, eases your mind as to the sort of man who has been forced to go without this past holiday?"

"I was afraid to bring it to the police myself, sir. A treasure like that and with all the stir in the papers these five days."

"Quite so. Well, I shan't detain you longer, Peterson. You've a roast goose waiting for you at home, and I've an impatient Yard inspector awaiting my own input upon this case. Leave the hat just there, thank you."

We saw our visitor out and turned our attentions back to the jewel which lay in state upon our dining table.

"My word, Holmes." Watson stared agog at the bauble. "Could it be that the Yard has got the wrong man? I thought, from the accounts in the papers, they had made an arrest five days ago."

I snorted. "And for that, I think we shall pay a visit to Lestrade before we go calling upon the Countess. Come along, Watson."

My words had arrested him in the act of putting on his own coat and hat. He turned to me now, his face positively beaming. "You wish me to come?"

"Yes, if you have nothing better to do."

Afterword

Sitting within our former lodgings at 221B Baker Street, I forbade Watson from ever making public our involvement in the case of Jack the Ripper. At the time, I chose that path, not only due to the personal nature of various aspects of the case—for myself and for him—but also as Watson's glowing treatment of fact and fancy might serve to remove from the case the true horror of the events in Whitechapel as well as my own failings in the investigation.

Now, in my later years, having seen the infamy Jack the Ripper did manage to secure for himself, I find it useful to at least have put to pen the efforts of those who were involved in the case, capturing as best I could the utter desperation of the police to put an end to that East End horror who stalked the night and the sheer evil of the man who had carried out such atrocious murders.

Lastly, I hoped, in my humble way, to memorialise those women who fell under the Ripper's knife.

As I had often told Watson, my search for justice was its own reward. In no other case within my lengthy career was this claim more true. For in no other case had the villain's knife come so near my heart.

- S. H.

APPEARANCES

In penning the story which you have now just read, I found myself poring over historical news accounts, inquests and articles, old photographs, and maps of the city of London. I became intimately familiar with the people whose lives were touched by the actions of Jack the Ripper. Pulling together the manuscript for editing, I was tasked with making a list of all named characters within the story. Upon doing so, I saw with fresh eyes what, exactly, I had managed to do and so it is incumbent upon me to share with you the 'who was who' as set within the larger frame of fact and fiction. In the following list, * indicates an actual historical figure and, unless otherwise noted, hard facts presented within the story are accurate from contemporaneous sources. (Characterization, however, is my own.) A second symbol † indicates a Sir Arthur Conan Doyle canon character. (Every possible step was taken to ensure accuracy of character, motive, history, and fact as conceived by Sir Arthur Conan Doyle. Sharp eyed 'irregulars' will

have enjoyed many little nuances – including but
certainly not limited to such esoteric touches as
which particular pipe Holmes chooses in chapter
21.)

Main characters:

Sherlock Holmes[†] - the world's only
consulting detective

John Watson[†] - hardly needs an
introduction but his placement at
the outset of the story is recently
married (to former client Miss
Mary Morstan) and no longer
living at 221B Baker Street

Detective Inspector Lestrade[†] -
somewhat informally a friend of
Holmes and one of Scotland
Yard's most capable detectives

Mary Watson (Morstan)[†] - client in
the case of The Sign of the Four
and now wife to Dr. John Watson

Billy Wiggins[†] - head of Sherlock
Holmes' unofficial police street
force of children a.k.a. "The
Baker Street Irregulars"

Perth – one of the irregulars

Supporting:

Jack the Ripper* alias "Red Fiend" &
"The Whitechapel Murderer" –
(Please note that his actions,
motives, and demise are of my
own invention, done so as to give
closure to the case as interpreted
by this story but done with an eye

to not giving him voice, face, or agency.)

Hamish Watson[†] - character is confirmed in canon but first name is something that Holmesian historians have simply agreed upon (alternatively, the 'H.' in John H. Watson is sometimes believed to stand for 'Hamish' instead)

Mrs. Hudson[†] - endlessly patient landlady of 221B Baker Street and support to Sherlock Holmes' eccentric profession

Sir Charles Warren* - Commissioner of the Metropolitan Police

Inspector Joseph Chandler* - first man on the scene of Annie Chapman's murder

Doctor Phillips* - in charge of post mortem for Annie Chapman, physical description in story from an actual photograph

Mr. Louis Diemshutz* - discoverer of Elizabeth Stride's murder

Police Constable William Smith* - beat officer for Elizabeth Stride murder scene

Israel Schwartz* - probable witness of Jack the Ripper himself at the Elizabeth Stride murder scene

Doctor Sequeira* - doctor called to scene of Catherine Eddowes' murder

Sergeant Jones.* & Inspector Collard*

- first policemen on the scene of Catherine Eddowes' murder

Inspector Beck* - PC on the scene of Mary Jane Kelly's murder (Note: his words to Ins Dew are a historically accurate quote)

Inspector Dew* - PC on the scene of Mary Jane Kelly's murder

PC Long* - discoverer of Goulston Street clues

Detective Constable Halse* - manned the scene of Goulston Street graffiti

Tertiary figures:

Dr. Llewellyn* - doctor for Mary Ann Nichols' murder

John Pizer, nickname of "Leather Apron" * - briefly suspected of Annie Chapman's murder. Some records have his name as "Jack" but I've stuck with John throughout

Mr. Edward Stanley (nickname of "The Pensioner")* - additional suspect in the Annie Chapman murder

Mr. John Davies* - discoverer of Annie Chapman's body

Mrs. Richardson* - resident of 29 Hanbury

Doctor Gordon Brown* - doctor for Mary Jane Kelly's post-mortem

George Lusk* - leader of the

Whitechapel Vigilance
Committee

And lastly but never least,

Victims of Jack the Ripper:

Emma Smith*
Mary Ann Nichols*
Annie Chapman*
Elizabeth Stride*
Catherine Eddowes*
Mary Jane Kelly*

Lightning Source UK Ltd.
Milton Keynes UK
UKHW010729280722
406510UK00001B/223